# She knew she should resist him

His lips rested upon hers, making no effort to carry the caress to any conclusion. Unconsciously her body arched to meet his. An arm moved abruptly about her, a hand splayed against her back, bringing flesh to meet flesh, curve to meet curve.

No gentle butterfly touch was holding her attention now; nor was she being wafted away, either. She knew exactly what she was doing—and she didn't care. Her desires flew to meet those searching lips, unconcerned about consequences.

Then suddenly extraneous thoughts were gone. As she returned those slow heartbreaking kisses, on tiptoe, both arms about his neck, only a longing was there to be even closer, to be a part of this man holding her, kissing her.

# My Lord Kasseem

## Mons Daveson

# Harlequin Books

TORONTO • NEW YORK • LOS ANGELES • LONDON
AMSTERDAM • PARIS • SYDNEY • HAMBURG
STOCKHOLM • ATHENS • TOKYO • MILAN

Original hardcover edition published in 1982
by Mills & Boon Limited

ISBN 0-373-02534-3

Harlequin Romance first edition March 1983

# CHAPTER ONE

'My son!'

The tall figure standing by the long window over-looking the growth of vivid, prolific green was staring into the distance, seeing none of it. He was gazing beyond to where, not far away, he knew was the blazing heat of a desert, his mind grappling with per-mutations . . . with frustrations.

He turned, his hand going to forehead, lips, and heart, as he bowed in the traditional gesture of re-spect. The man who had entered the large cool room, looked him over, from the djibbah and volu-minous burnous, in pristine white, to the kaffiyeh, closely bound with a black and silver cord, falling about his face. The faintest of twinkles came into eyes that had worn seriousness when he entered.

'At least, my son, you are dressed for it—diplom-acy personified! However, there is an easier way of obtaining this money—you know that.'

'I know! And I might have to come to it, because I will use no more of our personal fortune. But the work is necessary if our country is to survive; our government realises that. Also, if we can perfect the system here, it can be used in Saudi. So they can well part with some of their easily come-by loot.'

'Untold amounts of that same loot would be forth-coming if you could see your way to contract that alliance with the Princess. . . .' The older man's voice stopped abruptly at the chopping motion of his son's hand.

'That is something I also know. I have been informed,' here, the dark eyebrows rose mockingly, 'more than once of that fact—oh, with the utmost of diplomacy I must admit, but I . . . I have only this one short life to live. Is it wrong for expectation to soar above the mundane, or is that just the consequence of my misbegotten double heritage? Oh, my father!' The young man in his spotless white bent in a lower obeisance than he had used in his greeting earlier. 'I didn't mean. . . .'

A hand went up to still the apology. 'Your brother manages quite well, however. Except that with more of our country's blood than you have, he prefers the West, while you. . . .'

'It's unfortunate for me that I don't prefer the West. It would offer fewer difficulties. Still,' the sombre eyes lightened, taking on a malicious gleam, 'we'll have to see what diplomacy can achieve. Wish me a silver tongue in the next two days.'

Before his father could reply, a servant had entered. He bowed, saying, 'The car is waiting below, my lord.'

## CHAPTER TWO

IT was vast, the echoing airport of Athens—much larger than the international airport at home in Brisbane. She turned an anxious glance on her companion. But Miss Maitland was lying back in her deep chair, eyes half closed, looking relaxed enough, but Alex knew better. The trip from Australia had tired her; and there was this one, too, that they were about to set out upon—to Egypt; to Cairo. Alex felt a shiver of excitement pass through her whole body.

To actually be going there; a place she had always dreamed of, but what was to her as far away as the moon. She smiled a small secret smile. Anyway, if they didn't manage to get away to Egypt, she had seen Athens—the Acropolis, the Parthenon. And . . . her little smile widened . . . she had seen the inside of a beautiful Greek church.

Her reflections halted. She listened to the blare of the loudspeaker and turned to the silent figure at her side, seeing that the eyes were open. 'It's ours,' Alex said. 'Another hour late. That will make it almost night-time when we get to Cairo.'

'I expect so. But as long as we get our business done and get home safe and sound, a few hours hanging around an airport doesn't matter.' The elderly upright form leant back again upon the padded chair rest, and Alex knew, having known her—even though not intimately—all her short life, the pain that must be there to make that straight back slump as it was doing.

The journey from Brisbane had been long, but disembarking had been easy: something that Alex had worried about, knowing that to manage this chore had been one of the reasons for her presence. Everyone seemed to speak English. Luggage cleared, taxi procured, and they had been quickly wafted to the King George V Hotel.

Receiving a bark in answer to a question, once they had been left alone in the beautiful room overlooking a huge square, Alex said, a little breathlessly, 'Look, Miss Maitland, I'll run a bath now. Come

along and climb straight into it. It will relax your
tired muscles. I'll unpack and order your dinner up
on a tray.'

'I'm not an invalid, I'll have you know,
Alexandra. I may be a little tired, but then, even
being so young, so should you be.' The voice was
curt, almost harsh, but the girl knew it was pain
that made it so. She smiled back at the lined face,
and put a hand under the arm nearest her.

'Yes, you're right—I am, dear Miss Maitland. But
do come now and have your bath.'

They walked the few steps to the bathroom door;
the heavy stick taking the weight on one side, Alex's
young arm the other.

'I'll run the water while you begin undressing.' A
plug was inserted, taps turned on. A quick return to
a suitcase had a nightdress flipped over the vanity
chair-back, and Alex said, 'Just soak and relax, I'll
get things shipshape inside.'

'You know, Alexandra, when I suggested you
come with me, I didn't expect I'd find myself
saddled with someone who appears to have gradu-
ated from a prison warders' seminar. I thought I
would have a nice young, sweet little girl, who
maybe might be useful as a nursemaid—if I ever get
this whole damn business sorted out, and there's a
necessity for such a person.'

'I haven't been to any warders' seminar, Miss
Maitland.' Crispness was in the girl's tone now. 'I
do want to conserve your energy and strength, and
help you when I'm able. After all, that's the main
reason I'm here, isn't it? The other is only supposition.'

'Oh, go away with you! Shut the door as you go.
I *can* bath myself, you know.'

Knowing that that bark was worse than its bite,

Alex pulled down the elaborate bedspread and
banked the pillows against the headrest. Then out of
one of the large suitcases she hung away a dress for
tomorrow's journey. Standing then for a moment
undecided, a knuckle up to her mouth, she crossed
to the telephone.

'Room service!'

'Would you send up a light dinner for one to Miss
Maitland's suite, please. Yes, something like that,'
she answered, to the accented voice suggesting soup,
and a sole Mornay, followed by fresh fruit. 'With
tea,' she finished, as an afterthought. Miss Maitland
didn't drink coffee.

Alex moved to the window overlooking the square.
It was after six o'clock, but still warm and bright
outside. And that outside was like a disturbed anthill.
Crowded footpaths with their hurrying throngs,
tables—in their hundreds, she suspected, trying to
take in the huge scene just down there below her
gaze. People milling about, greeting friends, forming
parties with chairs dragged from other tables. Men
in both severe business suits and casual clothes, their
heads together, solving the world's problems by the
looks of it. It was an exciting scene; different entirely
to home. The air appeared to hold ozone, heady,
intoxicating; the atmosphere, the unfamiliarity of a
foreign clime. But not as heady as where they were
off to tomorrow—a land whose history she had
imbibed and delved into from five thousand years
ago to the present day.

Reluctantly she turned away from the stirring
scene and went through the huge bedroom that was
Miss Maitland's, into her own smaller one next door.
Unlocking her one case, she withdrew and shook out
a jersey silk dress, that looked as if it had never seen

the inside of a closely packed bag, and slid the purply-blue creation upon a hanger. Thank goodness for synthetics! Adding briefs and bra, all that was necessary in this climate, she returned to the larger room, again to wait by the window.

Bath finished and helped into the wide bed, a light sheet pulled across her, pillows banked behind the head that sank back, Miss Maitland managed a token smile. She reached for the tablets Alex had placed on the night table.

'These will make a difference. Go and have your own bath now, Alexandra.'

'Okay. If there's a knock at the door, it will only be the waiter with your dinner. Tell him to come in.'

'Will I, indeed! It's incredible that the small, prettily behaved girl I used to see off to school with my niece has grown into you! Did I tell you that before? In my day, girls as young as you were looked after themselves, not taking on the management of a journey to outer civilisation, *and* the care of an old crock like me too, in their stride.'

'Dear Miss Maitland, if I didn't know better I'd begin to think you're sorry you brought me.' Her tone changing, Alex went on, 'But seriously, it's to save you the expenditure of effort that I'm here. I really am trying to do just that, and to get you home as well as we can ... and with as little pain as we can.' She flipped a hand, and departed bathroom-wards.

She had a shower, and washed out the wisps of underclothes, as she always did when travelling. *She* hadn't two great suitcases, and the automatic gesture of ringing for a laundress. Standing in front of the mirror, rubbing at the ends of her damp hair, she gazed at herself.

At the light blonde hair—oh, not the blondness that caused heads to turn. Just ordinary light hair, well kept and shining, that swung about her shoulders. Not even blue eyes did she have to go with it. Hers were a dark slate grey. But one attribute she thanked the gods for. Although her lashes were long, they were only a few shades darker than her hair— but her eyebrows; black, slanting in a crooked arch, swung outwards to her temples. The very unexpectedness of such a contrast in otherwise fair surroundings drew the attention immediately. And she didn't, she had more than once indignantly protested, colour them or shape them. They were natural.

Brushing that same hair absently, she remembered Miss Maitland's niece. Alex had lived in the street behind the Maitland home—huge, built in the last century, high on the hills at Clayfield, overlooking the Brisbane river. As long as she remembered—if she had remembered, or even thought about it—Miss Maitland had lived there alone with her niece.

Norma had gone to the same primary school as Alex, and had caught the same school bus. As the years passed and high school finished, Norma had drifted out of Alex's life, first to university and then to England, where she had fallen in love with Raschid. Now she was dead, leaving behind a little girl and a new baby.

Alex herself had taken a librarian's course, and had led the normal, uneventful life of any well-adjusted young girl, except that most of her pleasure came from reading; history for the most part. Her mother's death from a heart attack hadn't caused any deep grief. They had never been very close, respect on both sides being the main ingredient of their relationship.

But Miss Maitland had been kind. She would come into the public library, and although no chairs were left about, one was always procured for her. There would always be books found for her too. The girls all knew about the pain that made it hard for her to get about.

Alex hung the towel upon its rack, and began vigorously to brush her hair, her thoughts still on Miss Maitland. She wondered what would be the outcome of this journey that would end tomorrow in Cairo. Norma had met and married her Egyptian in London; her aunt had never met him, and though there had been parental opposition from both sides, Norma had gone blithely to Egypt with her Raschid. If she had ever regretted it, the fact had never shown. She had written ecstatic letters home to Miss Maitland, her only living relative, and love of her husband had coloured them all.

And later, love for a baby daughter had come to share the pages. Then, so Miss Maitland had informed Alex when she had asked her to accompany her on this journey, had come a miscarriage and finally another baby . . . which had lived, the woman sitting straight-backed in her chair had said curtly, but whose mother had died.

They wanted to see her, the lawyers had written—for what purpose she was unaware. Money, she supposed. Reluctant though she was to undertake the long journey to so foreign a land, nevertheless, duty had sent her preparing for it. She couldn't really think it was the children they wanted her to take, but how she wished it were. They were a part of Norma. She expected money was probably the reason, she had said a second time, and had closed her mouth firmly. Alex suspected there would be a great deal of that, remembering her companion's life-style.

Still—she gave a tiny shrug   none of that affected her. All she had to do was to take care of Miss Maitland to the best of her ability, to fetch and carry, and . . . she gave a little skip, to see all she could crowd in, as the days ahead went by. There would be memories to take home.

But it was with sedateness that she walked back into the large bedroom after finishing dressing, to see the waiter placing a tray upon a stand he had slid across the bed. He checked the dishes, placed a glass carefully where it wouldn't be jogged, gave another all-encompassing glance about it, then turned away.

'I've told them to look after you, Alexandra. Go now and have your own dinner, like a good girl.'

Alex moved towards the corridor door with the young man, smiled when he spoke his few careful words in English, and quite a few more in Greek. As he departed, she snipped back the lock and returned to the bedside.

'It looks nice,' she said. 'Try to manage it all. We have a big day ahead of us tomorrow.' She didn't say, we were hoping to go to the Acropolis. But it had been mentioned.

Smiling with anticipation at the thought of it, she flipped her hand and passed through her own door, and thence out to the corridor, locking the door behind her.

The lift went down with a swish, but entering the lounge, foyer, or whatever, Alex hesitated. It was

beautiful, she decided, gazing about her, an edifice
from a bygone age. Hotels weren't built like that
these days. This one had probably been erected for
the few, moneyed and leisurely. Today's hotels were
built for tourists—in their hordes, and why shouldn't
they be? Luxurious certainly, but not with the opu-
lence, the elegance, that gave to this room a graci-
ousness that encircled one.

Making her way across to the dining room, she
paused uncertainly just inside the entrance.

'Miss Pembroke?' It was the maître d'hotel. And
at her nod he answered, 'Come with me.'

Wondering at such attention, nevertheless she
followed his retreating back. He seated her and
handed her a menu.

Alex turned to him, handing it back. 'Could you
choose for me, please?' she asked. 'Not many courses,
but all Greek cooking, if you would.'

'Of course, mademoiselle, the best of our food.'
He waved a hand at a waiter hurrying to him, pouring out a flood of Greek. 'Enjoy your dinner, mademoiselle.' He gave a small nod and turned away to
welcome a group of four just arriving.

Gazing about her, Alex saw that the large room was
only sparsely populated. Probably much too early
for these continentals, she surmised. A glance at her
watch showed barely eight o'clock, and she was
almost finished. They would be just about to set out.

Unlocking the door of her own room, feeling
pleasantly replete with a meal that had turned out
to be an unqualified success, she flipped the light
switch, and walked softly across the carpet to the
slim opening of the connecting door. The room
showed only a dim illumination, which came, Alex
saw, from a night light in the far end of the room.

Miss Maitland was asleep, the tray gone, curtains pulled completely across the windows overlooking the square. To be asleep so soon, she must have taken one of the pills she took so seldom, Alex thought, backing out.

She drew the door almost shut again. The maid had been in here too. The bed was turned down, a nightdress she had thrown carelessly over the lid of her case was neatly spread across her pillow. Curtains covered the windows.

She couldn't really go to bed at this time of night, and she felt unlike reading. Restlessly she walked across to the window. Should she go out for a short walk? Athens was a law-abiding city, with police patrolling everywhere. Also English was almost a common language. Her shoulders lifted. She would ask the girl at the reception desk if it was a permissible thing to do.

'Well. . . .' replied this individual when appealed to, 'you should come to no harm, provided you stay around here in the lighted streets. I wouldn't,' here she looked Alex over, 'sit out there at a table alone. No one would molest you, but possibly there would be more than one who would try . . .' a pause, as if searching for words, 'to pick you up.'

'No!' Returning the smile as one between women, Alex told her, 'I've been around and can quite definitely take care of myself. The thing I was wondering, though, was—is there anywhere close to here from where the Acropolis can be seen?'

'There is, and it is really only a small distance. You walk along the front of the hotel, turn right at the first street, then left at the next intersection, and you will find yourself in a street that looks straight up to it. You simply can't get lost.' She turned to another guest, smiling at a question.

Okay, thought Alex. Acropolis, here I come! Out of the entrance she walked, and the warmth of a Greek summer hit her. Air-conditioning was all very well in its place, but—she took a deep breath of this foreign country's atmosphere with a pleasure that lit up her whole face.

Along past the façade of the King George V, turn right, the street paced off. Left! Alex went down the pavement lightly, then abruptly she was halted. She had come to a street that rose high on both sides, a tunnel that led straight to the Acropolis, standing high on its hill bathed in moonlight. Fantastic is an overworked word, but it was all Alex could apply.

She leant against the wall behind her, just absorbing, and was brought back to her surroundings by laughter close by. She turned. Three men—no, three youths, actually, were trying to attract her attention.

Alex smiled carefully, not at them but across their shoulders. And as they began to close in, friendly, but with the firm idea of engaging her attention, she sidled along the rough sandstone of the building behind and walked quickly along to a group of people emerging from a building. They were mostly women, some clothed all in black, and she was soon among them. She saw that it was a church from which they had emerged.

Thankfully, she halted and gazed over her shoulder, not really perturbed, but hoping the youths had gone. She didn't want to walk back to the hotel with them tagging along.

Behind her back one of them called out, and abruptly, out of the blue, there was a flurry of movement; a staccato outburst of Greek. From the centre of a closely gathered knot of women burst a little cyclone of fluttering black. This apparition fastened on to one of Alex's would-be cavaliers and was beating him across the head, the shoulders, any place she could get at.

Astounded, Alex just gazed, a great smile breaking out. This developed into helpless laughter as the tableau continued—a little old lady lambasting into one hapless youth, the two others jumping like roosters around them. Almost doubled up with mirth, uncontrolable laughter gushing from her, Alex wrapped her arms across her shaking figure.

Just about recovering as the violent activity subsided, she was set off again into almost hysterics, as the first unfortunate youth escaped; the second, who had been making some effort at rescuing his friend, was turned upon.

He took one look at the virago advancing upon him, then took to his heels, the third one following without more ado.

A quiet voice beside Alex said, 'He is her grandson. She says he should be at church, not accosting young ladies.' It was the priest addressing her.

She turned a face still lit up with laughter and he addressed her again. 'Would you care to see inside our church?'

'Oh, may I? I would like to.'

He moved away, sending a general smile going the rounds of his flock. Alex followed him in. It was beautiful! Used as she was to her own more austere Anglican house of worship, this seemed overwhelming. An aroma, whether of incense, or maybe perfumed oil that fuelled the small lights before icons, floated to her senses.

Standing at the back, she gazed out and across the brilliantly lit church, hearing the murmur of men's voices in what sounded like liturgy echoing back to her. She turned to leave, bobbing a half-curtsy of respect in the direction of the altar, and again found the priest by her side.

'My colleague is going your way,' he told her. 'Go in peace, *thespinis*.'

'Thank you.' As she marched homewards the memory of how he had addressed her brought a warm smile to her lips. *Thespinis* sounded so much more exotic than plain Miss.

Footsteps following merely paces away caused her to glance irritably behind her. A young priest was pacing sedately along. He raised a hand a little way with a shooing movement. Alex understood; she was to have an escort home.

A peep into the adjoining room, when she arrived, showed her companion still sound asleep. After undressing, Alex re-pulled the curtains which a maid had closed, allowing a faint light from the still crowded square to penetrate. Drowsily, as she lay curled comfortably up in bed, she thought of visiting the Acropolis tomorrow. What a thing to go to sleep on! But it wasn't that excursion she was dreamily aware of as oblivion came to overtake her. It was the scene that had reduced her to helpless laughter at three would-be Romeos being put to flight by a barely five-foot elderly female.

# CHAPTER THREE

BUT neither the Acropolis nor the Sacred Way was to echo to her footsteps the following morning. Miss Maitland was definitely unwell. Coaxed to eat a little breakfast, she drank some juice, sipped at her tea, and played with a crescent roll. She made no demur, either, when advised to rest back on her pillows until it was time to depart.

A soft knock at the door ushered in the receptionist Alex had spoken to last night. She brought with her a sheaf of papers—the account, tickets to Cairo validated, and a bundle of Egyptian currency. She also added as she turned to depart when her business was finished, 'A car will be waiting to take you to the airport at eleven. Your plane leaves just after twelve, but they like you to be early.'

So here they were, waiting. Alex settled down to watch the bustle of an international airport, and reminisce. Even if she hadn't walked the Sacred Way, the Pyramids were waiting . . . and Cairo . . . and Egypt. Dreaming, she was startled, when abruptly all about her was bustle.

'It's ours,' said her companion, making an attempt to rise. Alex bent quickly to help her.

'It's the time it takes to board these damn planes,' muttered Alex irritably, with another anxious glance at Miss Maitland. Once they had gobbled up their load, they certainly did the job they were built for. But the red tape necessary for that task to be accomplished. Oh well. . . .

Finally settled, Miss Maitland leant back with closed eyes, and Alex was free to talk if she wanted to, or gaze out of her window to see Athens and then the port of Piraeus cartwheel behind them. Then there was only the sea and white puffs of clouds.

It wasn't quite dark when Cairo at last spun beneath them. Low on the horizon was a bank of dull red where the sun had fired a passage on its way to bed for the night, and unbelievable was the volume of sound that greeted their arrival. The airport was packed, and for the first time hearing the incomprehensible speech loudly called all around them, Alex acknowledged that she was on alien soil.

Of course the dress helped that impression. Workers rushing about in their coffee-coloured djibbahs—desert Arabs, she surmised, garbed in white, noticing no one, as they moved around in groups. And Europeans of course were in evidence, dressed in both business suits and casual clothes. Walking slowly with her arm through Miss Maitland's towards the luggage roundabout, Alex nodded farewell to a group of American archaeology students who, luggage retrieved, waved as they departed. For a moment, Alex felt panic. These people, though from another country, were a known factor. Here. . . .

'We were to have been met! Where are they?' Fretfully her companion was saying for the third or fourth time.

'It doesn't matter, we'll manage.' If only those damn suitcases would appear on this contraption, Alex thought impatiently.

'Oh . . . oh!' handbag, book and magazines went crashing. An Egyptian hauling a suitcase from the moving belt, talking to a companion over his shoulder, had knocked Miss Maitland aside. Her stick flying a dozen yards away, she was already falling. Desperately trying to catch her, knowing in her panic what could happen to that fragile body, Alex yet knew in that split second that she would be too late.

Pushed aside by what felt like a rigid iron bar, her arms fell, and her face was enveloped in smothering folds of cloth and the aroma of sandalwood. She moved sharply and the enveloping fabric fell away. She saw then that a man, an Arab or an Egyptian, was setting Miss Maitland carefully upright. Alex's breath returned from somewhere low down in her diaphragm. What on earth had happened? It was Miss Maitland who had been sent flying; not her.

The folds of a kaffiyeh bound with black cord threaded with silver showed a face, dark, arrogant, that could have emerged from a painting five thousand years old. A hand belonging to that image rose, fingers snapped and pointed; Miss Maitland's stick was retrieved and handed to her.

Another figure had gathered up Alex's belongings. Accepting them, she drew a deep breath, endeavouring to come up with a formula to thank their rescuer. He neither looked at nor spoke to her.

'Your luggage?' It was a question.

'Alexandra has hers,' Miss Maitland was informing him. 'Mine is two large suitcases.'

Standing there amid all the bustle and cacophony of noise surrounding her, Alex felt flustered, entirely unlike her normal competent self. It didn't matter. A finger, dark, imperative, pointed. Two heavy suitcases were lifted; two figures in Egyptian clothes stood waiting. A burst of staccato Arabic, and her own case was added to the others.

'Aren't you being met?' The words were in English—completely assured English, as if it were no trouble to speak in that language, but they also carried the faintest of accents.

'We were to have been.' It was Miss Maitland again; the question being addressed to her. 'A firm of lawyers were to have had us met.'

'Their name?'

He gave no indication of being aware of them when he had the information. He must have given some indication, however, to his entourage, for they had picked up the luggage preparing to follow, before he began to make his way through the teeming, vociferous crowd.

Alex had deliberately moved to the far side of Miss Maitland, in an endeavour to put distance between the unexpected, unknown force which had so affected her—why, she didn't know. Nothing like this had ever been experienced by her metabolism before, and she wanted to dispense with it—entirely.

A hand was raised, and before it had fallen, a car had edged out of the traffic and pulled up beside them. A taxi, braking sharply, pulled in immediately behind, from which a young man tumbled. He turned at a run towards the airport entrance, then halted abruptly a few yards farther on and turned, his glance raking over Miss Maitland.

A hurried step back, his glance roving the group at the side of the long black car. It hesitated on the older woman, then on the immaculate figure clothed in white, who had remained immobile, making no effort to usher them into the car after the taxi's abrupt arrival.

The young man—for the newcomer was a young

Egyptian—stiffened. He bowed, not to them, but to their rescuing knight in shining cloth—not armour, thought Alex, the hysterical laugh trying to break through being sternly repressed. She didn't understand this encounter. She certainly didn't understand her own emotions concerning it.

A flood of Arabic issued from the tall, enigmatic, white-clothed figure. The young man bowed again and returned answer. Apparently it was of some moment, if his gesticulations were to be taken into consideration. A hand went up again, not to flip fingers, but to stay, and with sharp abruptness, what looked like more explanations.

'This young man is from your solicitors. His car was involved in an accident. It took some time to sort things out and to procure a taxi,' the clipped incisive, faintly foreign voice told them. 'He will now escort you to Shepheards Hotel.' He moved with every intention of departing.

Miss Maitland spoke, a hand held out. The desire of not wanting to be any more involved was so open, so apparent, that Alex wondered why. It cost nothing to accept thanks, wave them off, and be on one's way.

'May I thank you? I'm Miss Maitland. I've just arrived from Australia.' The man didn't touch the outstretched hand. He did, however, bow, raising hand to forehead, lips and heart, as Alex had seen done in films.

'This is my young friend Alexandra Pembroke. Mr . . .?'

This time he didn't give the Arabic greeting. Probably kept for superiors and the old, thought Alex. He merely bowed. But suddenly, so unexpectedly that she stepped back a half-pace, he looked at her, for the first time. Before, his glance had not merely slid over her, it simply had not encountered her, she might never have been present.

Darkness, already imminent, flared unexpectedly into brightness, as switched-on sodium lights poured their illumination everywhere. And in it Alex saw his eyes suddenly pinpointed with brilliance. Her own gaze held. She could no more look away than move. For the space of seconds, but what seemed to her eternity, neither spoke; the girl held by a pulse, a magnetism, flowing to her from that tall, white-clad stranger. Then the tableau was shattered. The man had entered the open door of the big opulent car, and with no sound at all that the bemused girl could hear, it had departed.

Their luggage bestowed in the taxi, they were seated in the rear of it. 'You will forgive my lateness, no?' Their new escort had turned, his arm across the back of the front seat. 'I am Ali.' He laughed, happy now that everything was in order. 'My proper name is hard to say, so I am Ali. I am to escort you to the hotel and come for you tomorrow. Ten o'clock, you understand me?' The young smooth face regarded them anxiously.

'Yes. Ten o'clock tomorrow morning. To take us to your firm's office.'

Ali nodded happily.

'Tell me, Ali,' asked Miss Maitland, 'who was the gentleman who helped us just now?'

'Good!' muttered Alex under her breath. 'Just what I wanted to know but couldn't ask.'

For a minute it appeared the question was going to remain unanswered. The youth had turned purposely back to the front again.

'Ali!' There was no mistaking the tone in Miss Maitland's voice.

Back towards them again, Ali's face didn't register happiness now. He shrugged, giving the universal action of not understanding.

'Nonsense, of course you know him—or of him!' Almost a bark was in the older woman's voice. It brought Ali up short. This was his employer's client.

Shoulders rose in a different kind of shrug this time. 'He is the Sheik Kasseem ben Omair. Very wealthy, very powerful. . . .' A desperate unwillingness to continue the subject showed.

Alex wondered if he were a politician, or . . . an emptiness engulfed where her stomach should be. He couldn't be a criminal! Not that composed, assured, arrogant stranger. But criminals, rich ones *were* assured, arrogant. But he wasn't; somehow she knew that.

'Is he an Egyptian?' Miss Maitland's words broke in upon her reverie.

Ali's face dissolved into a state of misery again. 'Yes . . . no . . . an Arab, from the desert. Not like to talk about the Sheik Kasseem ben Omair.' This time he definitely ended the subject, client or no client. He talked to the driver in his own tongue, words spilling over one another in his haste.

Settling back, Alex gazed out at this alien city. They were travelling a wide, straight road, apparently going on for ever, strange, exotic. Egyptians walked along on both sides in their long coffee-coloured gowns. Occasionally there were figures in the flowing white she had just been made familiar with. And cars. . . . It was incredible. She had thought of Egypt as slow-moving, camel-orientated. There were more motor vehicles here than in

Brisbane in peak hour, all going like bats out of hell
too. And the noise! There was certainly more of that
than at home. All these impressions were only surface
ones, she knew. What she was really thinking of was
an Arab . . . from the desert. He was dark enough to
spend his days there, but his face was lean, austere
almost. Of course, all that she had actually seen of
him was part of a face between that so white kaffiyeh
. . . and fingers that had snapped and pointed.
Abruptly she was flung forward as, with a surge and
the slamming on of brakes, they arrived.

Ali was out of the taxi, the door opened. A porter,
or some such servant, in the now-familiar coffee
djibbah, was also there, two others, each carrying
part of their luggage, had moved up the few steps.

Inside, immense, the foyer stretched on all sides—
vast high ceilings, marble floor that struck cool to
one's feet. It had also, in its huge centre, a design,
intricate, colourful, that drew attention immediately. A craftsman long ago had certainly laid
it, like an expensive Persian rug: Alex walked over it
with compunction.

So this was Shepheards Hotel, remaining from
when Britain ruled in Egypt. Well, some outstanding
legacies had been left behind.

'Are you all right?' anxiously she asked her companion. 'Shall I take you over to that couch to sit
down?' Miss Maitland didn't look at all well, and
they were standing waiting just inside the office reception area. It was a crowded reception area.
Apparently they had struck what would be called a
convention at home. Arabs, Egyptians—Alex
shrugged, not knowing if they were one and the
same, except that Ali had seemed to differentiate—
milled about in their flowing robes. European suits

were not absent, either, which even to her inexperienced eye cried Saville Row or Brooke Brothers.

Ali was trying to attract the attention of one of the two men behind the large reception desk. These men seemed no ordinary clerks, they were talking and laughing with the would-be guests as if meeting friends of their own, checking reservations and handing out keys. It looked as if they would be in for a long wait. Then Alex saw Ali, with a further anxious glance at Miss Maitland, call loudly again to one of the clerks, who spoke shortly back. Even in another language, and from this distance, that he was being told to wait was plain to her. They were busy.

Their escort replied, more emphatically—the word Sheikh, and could it have been ben Omair. Why would he use that name? It had nothing to do with them.

It was funny, she thought, funny strange, not funny ha-ha, but almost immediately silence came to take the place of what had been nearly pandemonium. It was uncanny. A clerk spoke sharply. Ali answered, his demeanour almost frightened, and Alex suddenly found their small group the cynosure of all eyes. A book on the desk was swung round, some keys lifted from their slots, and one of the men had left the desk and was moving towards them.

'Miss Maitland, Miss Pembroke,' he was holding out keys to their ankle-clothed attendants, 'we apologise for the delay, but we have been inundated, as you can see.' His arm went out with a throw-away gesture to the large group still facing their way.

'Anything you need, just ask your porter along your corridor. The station is always manned. The dining room is at the top of the hotel, not down here, and dinner is whenever you want it. I hope you will be comfortable.' He gave the smallest of half-bows and turned away. They followed their departing luggage across the beautiful marble floor, Ali bringing up the rear.

'What was all that about, Ali?' Alex asked him.

'Only very busy,' he shrugged. And gazing at the deliberately blank expression he turned on her, she knew she would get no more out of him on the subject.

Along the deep-carpeted corridor on the fifth floor, they followed their guide, and pausing at one door, her porter moved on to the next. It wasn't to be a connecting suite this time, then. A small ante-room received them, then a large bedroom with glass doors opening on to a balcony. Alex promised herself to explore her own view as soon as possible.

'Do you know, Alexandra, I know I should be feeling done-up, but I feel remarkably well,' said Miss Maitland, as they looked about them. 'Do you think it might be the climate? There's hardly any pain.'

Alex laughed. 'Oh, come on! You haven't been here long enough, but isn't it marvellous that you're feeling better?'

'It is, and you know what I'm going to do? I'm going to get dressed and go up to dinner at this famous hotel. Deal with these men,' Miss Maitland, added, pointing, as they waited by the door. Alex had been given a roll of Egyptian pounds before they left Athens with the admonition. 'They tell me, Alexandra, that it's necessary, or rather the custom, to tip everywhere in Egypt, so use your discretion.'

Alex had never tipped in her life before, but with the appearance of a seasoned trouper, she withdrew two of the bills from the zipped compartment in her handbag, handing one to each. It must have been satisfactory. She received smiles and a nod, and followed by Ali, they departed.

'Well,' Alex grinned at her companion, 'every new experience is a broadening influence, they say. Now, can I help here. Unpack or run your bath?'

'No, you can't. I'm perfectly capable of taking care of myself tonight. Run along and prepare yourself for dinner. Give me half an hour.'

Alex went, if not running, she went on dancing feet. This was Egypt, and the Nile was right outside her bedroom balcony.

The river the Pharaohs had sailed upon in their golden barges! In through her own small hallway and out through the glass doors she danced, shutting the glass behind her to keep the air-conditioning viable. On the balcony, if not monarch of all she surveyed, at least it was something to romance over.

As she watched the sails of a felucca as it parted the moonlit silver water in midstream, her thoughts went to a man, an Arab. What would he be doing now? she wondered. Certainly not thinking about her. He was a part of all this, of that passing parade strolling along a kind of promenade that wended along the river's edge. Of men in their flowing robes, of men also dressed in Western clothes, and of occasionally, a boy and girl. Well, at least, that was something. There were couples walking together, and they were Egyptians too, she noted.

Reluctantly she turned away. She must bathe and get up to dinner. In lemon cotton, cool scooped-neck and sleeveless, she smoothed an oil-moistened finger over her eyebrows, settling them to lie arched and extended, giving to eyes that were merely commonplace, a mystique all of their own. The lightest application of lipstick followed; a quick brushing of her golden hair, and she went to the room next door.

'Ready?' she asked.

'Yes.' Retrieving her stick and handbag from the bed, Miss Maitland spoke. 'You know, Alexandra, this country is where Norma lived for almost six years. She did mention it in her letters, but it was love of her husband that was the mainspring of her life, not the country. It doesn't do anything for me, either. I just want to get my business done and get home.'

Moving along the deep-carpeted corridor to the lifts. Alex kept silent. She knew it would be no hardship for her to live in this land. Everything would not be perfect, she acknowledged that, but the place had laid its spell upon her.

The dining-room spread out before them, long and deep, colourful with its waiters in their ankle-length gowns, its maître d'hotel in crimson jacket and black narrow cut trousers. It was this man who came to greet them.

'Miss Maitland, Miss Pembroke—I've sat you by a window.' His gaze waited upon the older woman, but passed to the girl's sparkling, eager face, and his own expression changed from the politeness of service to a genuine smile.

A waiter in the now familiar coffee-coloured djibbah took charge of them. They dined leisurely, Miss Maitland eating more than her usual frugal meal, Alex noted, pleased. But although it was a colourful, exotic crowd surrounding her, Alex's gaze was drawn to the windows merely a hand's stretch away. Covered by a light flimsy orange chiffon, the curtains did nothing to hide the myriad lights of the city stretching as far as the eye could see. And the cars—did they never stop?

She mentioned them to their crimson-jacketed supervisor who was constantly patrolling among the tables.

'But you see,' he smiled down into the questioning face, 'we get our petrol from our brothers in Saudi Arabia. One day maybe,' here a shrug lifted the crimson shoulders, 'we might be able to pipe our water from the mighty Aswan dam and return it for their oil. Have you been up to Aswan?'

It was Miss Maitland who shook her head. 'No, I don't expect we'll get there. I'm limited in my travels.'

'A pity! Still, if you miss Aswan, you might go to Luxor. It also has so many magnificent sights to see.' He nodded, and went along on his checking.

'I think I'll go to bed now, Alexandra. I wish you could go out a bit more—still, after meeting these pushy lawyers tomorrow, we'll hire a guide and let you see something of the place. You really can't be expected to go home without seeing the Pyramids, can you?' The smile she turned on Alex as they crossed the dining-room ante-room to the lifts held wicked mischief.

'I wouldn't want to, Miss Maitland, but it's all in your hands,' Alex replied sedately, and was rewarded with a chuckle.

There was a bar in the far corner of the ante-room, occupied by quite a large group. Men in their voluminous, immaculate white robes, and head-dresses—like the one at the airport, went immediately through her mind—mixing with Western-clad business men. She wondered if that was the group who had arrived just as they did.

'I'll help you get ready for bed,' Alex was busy finding a nightdress, setting slippers, ready. . . .

'Good God, Alexandra, stop fussing! I'm perfectly well tonight—in fact, I can't believe how well. Now, be off with you, child. You shouldn't mind an early night yourself. We have been constantly travelling. The jet lag must catch up with us sometimes.

In her own room, Alex decided the so-called jet-lag hadn't caught up with her yet. She felt restless. Closing the glass doors behind her, she folded her arms on the protective railing of her little balcony and gazed across at the Nile, where not only the golden barges of the Pharaohs had sailed. Merchants too had used it to carry spices and precious metals. Armies also had made use of its far-flung waters for transport, both for war and pleasure. What stories it could tell!

Why shouldn't she just go down and walk a few hundred yards along it? She had in Athens. Common sense told her this was not Athens. This was an Eastern land, with very different standards. Of course she shouldn't go out alone. But what harm could a tiny walk get her into? It wasn't as if the promenade was deserted; women as well as men seemed to be walking there. And it wasn't late.

Quickly, before more sensible reflections could deter her, she moved inside. She wouldn't take her key, or her handbag with its money and passport. She wouldn't have to worry about anything then, just have a short walk up and down in front of the hotel.

Pulling the unlocked door to behind her, smiling at the porter at his little table, she marched to the lifts. This time she swished downwards. Out across the vast marble floor she went, wondering if she was being looked at. The place was crowded with guests from both sides of the world.

Swiftly past the group of taxi-drivers and guides, always at their station beside the hotel, she walked, then, awaiting a break in the traffic, across the road, and on to her goal.

No one spoke to her. No one molested her, and gaining confidence, she strolled along, hands in the pockets of her cotton dress, gazing at what looked like a mirror of beaten silver.

She didn't see the white-clothed native who, stepping from a launch moored at a jetty farther back along the river, halted abruptly as he sighted the slim figure crossing to walk so unconcernedly along. A hand went up to gain light upon a wrist watch; a muttered expletive followed, and the figure turned, hurrying along after the strolling girl.

Thinking it was about time she made for home, Alex began to turn, hands in pockets still, eyes on a set of sails skimming past her. Four youths in the long cotton gowns of their homeland, gesticulating, calling to each other as they hurried, were upon her as she turned. Unpremeditated, unnoticed, a knock caught her as she was turning. She stumbled and fell—under the top railing, on to a ledge which here ran high above the water.

# CHAPTER FOUR

No one had noticed her fall; above they were still hurrying about their own affairs. Alex found herself floundering in softness. The material was all over her, and the more she tried to extricate herself, the lower into it she sank: and enveloping the whole atmosphere around came a smell, a stench. Terrified now, as this new element became more powerful, she felt panic begin to build.

'Keep still! Keep still, I say!' She heard the words, but took no notice of the message. Her reaching hands towards the sound were slapped away. 'Just keep still, I told you.' This time the words did penetrate.

Hands under her arms lifted her. She found herself standing on solid ground beneath the promenade walk.

'Don't,' the voice spoke again as her hands went out to him. 'Just come with me along here. You can't go up on to the path in that condition. Be careful and follow my footsteps. Wait!' The last word echoed.

'Keep still!' A handkerchief scrubbed across her mouth and nose, and not gently either. She tried to speak of the place into which she had fallen.

'Look, Alexandra, don't speak. Don't do anything but follow me.'

No thought of not doing so occurred. Alex trod behind that fluttering white ghost, trying not to stumble on rough ground, or fall into declivities, on this, to her, nightmare journey. Lights from the street lamps were suddenly illuminating the surrounding night, and she saw they had come to a jetty where a boat was moored.

A sharp sentence in Arabic echoed.

A form materialised above them; another sentence came, and the figure moved away to return almost immediately.

'Take off your shoes. Don't put your foot upon the ground, place it into this slipper.'

Wondering what on earth this was all in aid of, almost in tears, Alex nevertheless obeyed that tone. First one shoe came off and then the other, and she was standing there in slippers.

'Put them in this,' the voice enjoined her. Gingerly she dropped her lovely sandals, bought for this trip, into the gaping mouth of a plastic garbage bag. A hand at her back propelled her up the gangplank on to the launch, then down steps and through a doorway. In bright light she saw that she was in a bathroom.

'Remain there a moment,' the voice of their rescuer from the airport said, and still shaken by the panic of being unable to extricate herself from the vile-smelling stuff into which she had fallen, Alex kept rigidly still.

He took a towel, she heard him turn on a tap, and then he poured liquid into his cupped hands. The strong taint of carbolic pervaded the room as he washed, while Alex stood dazed, wondering where she had ended up, and what she was doing here, and worse, looking as she did before this man. Why hadn't he just sent her back to the hotel?

Take the slippers off and stand in the bath. As she

glanced from the clouded, swirling water to the dark alien face, the thought of refusing and going home occurred. But her movement released again the sickening odour from off her person, so, shrugging, she put one foot after another over the bathtub, then dropped the slippers also into the held-out bag.

'Now, your clothes!'

That did end some of her lethargy.

'My clothes?'

Impatience coloured the tone now. 'I don't know what you fell into, but all kinds of people sleep out under the ledge of the river bank, despite the rigid bans of the authorities. It might even only have been an illegal felucca load of produce left too long. But whatever it was, innocuous or harmful, you can't take the chance. Get into the water and scrub yourself all over. Now, your clothes! Into the bag!'

She looked helplessly up at him, standing tall and alien and demanding. She saw the lines on that face begin to harden, brows beginning to meet over an aquiline nose in a thunderous expression.

'My good girl!' The words weren't thunderous, they were soft, but somehow that very softness, with the threat implicit behind it, galvanised her into obeying. 'Surely you don't imagine this is the prelude to a rape scene? For that, wouldn't you expect beautiful music, soft lights—and, I might add, a perfume more sweet than this stench?' He gestured both to the antisepticked water in which she stood and her clothes from which the nauseating aroma emanated.

Face burning at the tone, Alex pulled off the once pretty lemon dress, discarding it too into the bag he held out. Another glance at that hard, impersonal countenance, and she turned her back. Unhooking the scrap of nylon and lace, slipping off the equally brief bikini, she sent them on their way to meet the rest, dropping down into the water as she did so.

'Scrub your hands first, then turn off the taps.' The words were flung over a shoulder as he departed.

She scrubbed her hands, her fingernails, and then her body completely. Before she could begin to think about her rescuer, the intimidating presence was back, in his hands a container.

'Bend your head back!' he told her, and as it remained in the same position, the owner of it gazing blankly up at him, ungently he took a handful of hair and bent her neck back. It was carbolic water mixed with soap that was poured all over it, and powerful fingers thoroughly massaged her hair, ears, forehead—the lot.

'There, that should do it.' The tone held a different nuance from any she had before heard through it. And so it should! she thought wrathfully. She must look like a drowned rat sitting there—hair every which way tangled about a face scrubbed naked and red with carbolic, smelling like goodness knows what, being bathed like a recalcitrant two-year-old, when this was one time she would have given her ears to be glamorous, beautiful, groomed and lovely. Damn! Damn!

'Pull the plug now and get under the shower.' The voice tinged with amusement as it resumed. 'And here's something that goes more with a rape scene than carbolic.' A bottle came over her shoulder to drop into the water. A door shut decisively and she was alone.

Rescuing the container, she saw that it was shampoo, and, with a famous name brand upon it at that.

Well, well . . . obviously more than the masculine sex used the boat.

Lifting the plug, she stood, liberally using shampoo, allowing the extravagant river of soap bubbles to stream over her body. Finally she stood under the cold jets to rinse off, and flinging back her hair, wrung it out in a twisted coil.

From the bathmat, her glance roved till it alighted upon a bathtowel the size of a small sheet. Dry, a turban wound her head, she stood, wondering about clothes, then saw a white towelling wrap hanging on a hook from the door.

Too bad if it hadn't been left for her. She tried it on. It was a man's gown, and came to just above her ankles. Fastening it tightly around her middle by its cord, she began to rub her hair. Ten minutes and some vigorous action found it almost dry. Alex ran her fingers through its tangles trying to provide some semblance of order. She opened the door. It led into what she took to be the stateroom of the launch, and as she hesitated, her rescuer entered it from the opposite side.

Formally dressed once again in the djibbah, kaffiyeh, and burnous, that would be, Alex suspected acidly, uncontaminated by the least germ, she had yet to acknowledge that against anyone he would be outstanding. She dropped her gaze from that handsome, aloof countenance, unwilling for him to see the effect his presence had upon her.

'If you will come with me, Miss Pembroke, you can use my stateroom for the night. . . .'

Aghast, she interrupted, 'What do you mean—for the night——?'

'I meant precisely what I said.' Harshness had come to take over politeness, a prince of this land addressing a peasant. 'If you would care to make your entrance at Shepheards Hotel clad in my dressing gown, please say so, and Mustafa will escort you.'

'Oh, lord!' She hadn't thought that far. Stupid! Of course she would have to have clothes.

'Can't you get me something now . . . anything . . .?' The words trailed away. Where could someone like him get women's clothes at this hour? What on earth was she to do?

His hand came up, and a frown was again between those eyebrows after a quick glance at his watch. 'I'm late already—I must go. It's more than important. My attendance is imperative.' His finger beckoned as he turned away.

Perforce Alex followed. At a white-painted door, he stood aside. Passing him to enter, she gave no glance about her, only turned, meaning to importune once again. The man had moved too. Face a mere two inches from that pristine white linen, so fine it could almost be muslin, she remained there, rooted.

She had felt this emotion, this attraction, for no other man. She knew she should move away. She knew, of course she did, that she was courting anything that might happen. His behaviour had been impeccable. Even as these thoughts were coursing through her mind, she lifted her eyes to his face.

As at the airport, she saw again that brilliance. And, she thought in confusion, the eyes were not black as she had thought. They were hazel . . . no, they were green.

Then she was not wondering about colour. That head came down, and lips rested upon hers, slowly, staying there, making no effort to carry the caress to any conclusion; almost as if it were waiting. Unconsciously, her body arched to meet his. An arm was abruptly about her, a hand spreadeagled against her back, bringing flesh to meet flesh, curve to meet curve. No gentle butterfly touch was holding her attention now; she wasn't being wafted away, either. She knew exactly what she was doing, and she didn't care. Her desires flew to meet those searching lips, uncaring about consequences. Then suddenly, extraneous thoughts were gone. As she returned those slow heartbreaking kisses, on tiptoe, both arms about his neck, only a longing was there to be even closer, a part of this man holding her, kissing her. .

Shock at being set so abruptly, so rudely, away from him caused her whole body to arch backwards. His violent expletive echoed in Arabic, but Alex had no difficulty distinguishing the name of Allah. She was picked up, and corded, teak-hard arms carried her across the room, depositing her, not gently, upon the bed. Eyes that she had thought were green, but which with the light now behind them looked fathomless in dark sockets, gazed upon her, from her flushed rosy face, tangled, still not dry hair, to the dishevelled towelling gown, gaping untied, leaving no part of her to the imagination.

His arms rigidly imprisoned her on either side as they took his leaning weight, and moved. One to gather her to him, the other resting at the open neckline. Her own eyes, dazed, expecting, waiting, for what she didn't know, closed, as his mouth came, not to rest upon hers, but upon her temple. It trailed slowly, oh, so slowly, downwards. He felt the shiver, the shudder, convulsing her supine body, as it went even farther to rest upon the exposed swelling of whiteness. This—this is my reason for existing.

Somewhere in the back of her mind the words were flowing, not conciously, nothing was conscious to her, but those hands, those lips, that sent soaring the pulse of ecstasy into her bloodstream.

'Hell and damnation! What a time. . . .' Almost flung back upon the pillows, Alex lay shaken, as he swung round to stand with his back to her, tension in every line of his tall body. Then unexpectedly, the thought struck. He spoke in English! He must have been thinking in English!

'I've got to go,' he said, the strain in his voice when he had left her and sworn changed now to harshness. He made for the door without glancing her way. Alex rose in one swift movement and followed.

'Please. . . .' An arm outstretched entreatingly. 'I. . . . You must know. . . . I haven't. . . .' He did turn to look at her then.

'You don't imagine that I myself do this sort of thing all the time, either? As for you—give me credit, Alexandra, for some experience. I'd know, of course I would, if our lovemaking of just now was familiar territory to you. Look, I really must go.' He moved again to the door.

'Please. . . .' she said again. 'What do I call you?' She knew what Ali had told them, but how did one address an Arab sheikh?

The green eyes gazed frowningly at her for the briefest moment, then. 'Go to bed, Alexandra. I'll see you in the morning. Mustafa will be outside, and there are guards on the launch.' Another impatient glance at that wretched watch, she thought, and he was gone.

Alex didn't go straight to bed. She walked over to the dressing table, and what met her gaze in the mirror brought shock spilling over. Heavens, she looked like something from the centrefold of *Playboy*! Pulling the towelling gown fully closed, she tied the belt as tight as it would go. Brushes were on the ledge before her—plain, silverbacked—no engraving, no frills. She couldn't bring herself to use them, but she did reach for a slender comb that could have been anybody's. Dragging it through the tangled mass about her face, she did wonder what, if any, sort of hair dwelt within that kaffiyeh.

Slowly bringing her hair into some sort of order, then thinking back, she wondered why he hadn't accepted what had been his to take—and it had been. Crimson came to flush her face with colour at the thought that he might not have wanted to. Then common sense came to her aid. He *had* meant them, those kisses, those caresses. That she knew, even if she had to be credited with no experience.

The comb laid gently down, she flicked out the light and went to kneel on the bed. Outside the porthole, the water slid on its silent way, still bathed in silver from a moon not yet down. A sail came into her vision on the far side of the river—going where? she wondered.

She dropped down, reaching to pull the sheet about her. Plain linen sheets, not a vestige of silk or luxury about the place. If he had a harem, or even a wife, there was no sign of femininity on this boat, except for the shampoo that could actually have been his own.

Would he come here when he returned? How would she get her clothes to go back to the hotel? How. . . . Well, she couldn't do anything about that now. She would have to wait and see and try not to think too much of the minutes just past, of a touch that had sent pulses clamouring, of a desire to just belong. Alex had no intention of sleeping, and didn't know when conscious thoughts slipped into dreams.

She didn't know, either, when in the early hours of the morning soft footsteps walked up the gangplank, and a voice spoke as quietly in Arabic to a reclining figure posted there. The handle of her door turned, and it was pushed gently inwards. She didn't see the entering form place plastic shopping bags upon the chair and then move across to look down upon her. No *Playboy* image greeted him this time. The towelling gown was belted tight, the sheet loosely covering her.

He stood for some minutes, eyes sombre, then moved softly over the carpet and closed the door.

The light of a dawn just breaking was sending misty greyness through the porthole when Alex's eyes came open. Perplexed, she looked about the unfamiliar small compartment. Then remembrance hit, and her body came upright with a jerk. Kneeling on the bed, she glanced out of the small round window. The river was beginning to come alive wth the day's traffic. She raised a wrist to see the time—and remembered where the watch was now. Probably burnt to bits in some incinerator.

A knock sounded quietly on the door, and she swung round, eyes suddenly enormous. The sound came again, and she slid off the bed, calling, 'Come in!'

Her apprehension was unnecessary. It was Mustafa who gingerly opened the door only a little way.

'Lady,' he said, bowing, 'my lord says, dress. To go away early before many peoples are about.'

'Dress? But how, Mustafa . . .?' Her words trailed

off. The youth was pointing to some parcels lying
upon the chair.

'One quarter of the hour, lady, my lord says.'

The aperture was empty, the door closed.

'Oh, does my lord say!' muttered Alex acidly. He
could have come and told her himself. Nevertheless,
she moved quickly across and emptied the packages
out on to the bed.

'Gracious!' the exclamation came, as bra and
bikinis in material that was certainly not nylon were
revealed. She fingered silk that slid between her
fingers—and they were her size, she saw. Well, well.
The dress was again her size, she noted sardonically,
thinking acidly that he must know a great deal about
feminine measurements—or he knew someone who
did.

The dress was a creation—muted grey, that hung
loose from a yoke to swing in a flare to just below
the knees. Only the merest hint of cyclamen relieved
its plainness. Slipping on the undergarments, Alex
dropped its smoothness over her head, easing it about
her, seeing the flaring elegance swing, then settle in
folds. Even the colour was right; it drew no attention
as a bright colour would. And only other women
knowledgeable in such things would guess at its
origin and price. Certainly, Alex had never worn
something that was an original before.

Half out of the third cellophane bag, white sandals
showed, open-toed and ankle-strapped, brought
probably because that style would fit most girls her
size. She trod into them and fastened the strap. At
the dressing table, her hand again passed over the
silverbacked hairbrushes to take up the comb. A few
strokes and her hair was in order; the short fringe
lying straight. But it hung in a swathe across her

cheeks. The side-combs she normally used to keep it tidy in the daytime had gone the way of all her yesterday's belongings.

As satisfied as she could be without recourse to any make-up at all, she wandered over to the bed and took up the towelling robe. Folding it with caressing fingers, she placed it gently on the pillow. In years to come, she knew that just to see a gown like it would trigger back memories of the Nile, and a launch that rode its waters. The man who owned it was something else. What was it that had surfaced in her mind last night in the maelstrom of emotion which had engulfed her—something about a reason for existing? Yes; a wry smile etched itself about her mouth. In the short space of twenty-four hours a life could be changed.

But this was daylight, and the man was an Arab. And to men of his nationality respectable women didn't act as she had done. Her breath came in sharply . . . yes, the softest of knocks sounded again. She didn't call, 'Come in.' She went to open it.

Dressed as yesterday, in the whitest of robes, the kaffiyeh that left only half of his face showing, he addressed her gravely. 'Good morning. They fitted, I see.'

Behind the impassive face was there amusement? This thought enabled Alex to answer without the apprehension with which she had gone to meet him.

'Yes, indeed they do. Does that show the experience you informed me you had, or was it just the pick of the draw?'

'I'm afraid neither on this particular occasion. I have a friend who owns a department store. Being routed out at two o'clock in the morning to go down, unlock it, and choose for me what I wanted, was not

a situation he was particularly happy wth. But . . .'
amusement was hiding somewhere, 'there might
come a time . . . you understand?'

Yes, she could understand. This man could always
repay favours.

'Now, you must leave. Mustafa is busy outside.
He will see you off.' He stood aside for her to pass
him.

'Please,' Alex's hand went out, 'what do I do
about these clothes? I don't know what to say to
you. Can I be allowed to pay for them?'

'It is time for you to leave! Come along.' He
hadn't deigned to reply to her question. 'But one
thing,' he added, 'don't go out alone again. The
hotel will always provide a guide who will be re-
sponsible and registered.'

'I was only walking along a perfectly respectable
promenade looking at the Nile. . . .' Her indignant
rebuttal was waved away. He again motioned her
forward.

'Please. . . .' repeated Alex. 'Will I see you again?
Will you tell me what to call you?' How did one
address an Arab sheikh, even if one did know his
name?

'I will tell you my name the next time I see you.
Now, come along.'

From questioning, from distress at not knowing
how to further this acquaintanceship, her whole face
lit up, radiance giving brilliance to her eyes, a pink
flush of happiness to her cheeks. 'Will I . . . shall we
meet again? All right then, I'll go at once.' She
dropped a small curtsey, adding with a sidelong
glance up into the grave face, 'Thank you, my lord,'
and fled past before he could answer.

Mustafa was half way along the small gangplank,

busy flapping a blanket, and as it flapped Alex had moved past him and was on the promenade, yards from the launch. She didn't walk briskly, she strolled, which was what she would normally do when out for a walk. She passed Shepheards, then, a shudder rippling through her, was unable to make herself continue on to where she had gone under the railing.

A swift turn and she glanced up at her own balcony. The curtains were still pulled, but Miss Maitland's were open. Before she crossed to enter the hotel, she turned to look over the water. The sun just above the horizon was painting the Nile with gold. Sails from feluccas as they skimmed along showed like gulls' wings, sheer and flaring wide.

Pausing a moment, Alex drew a deep breath, then with a straight back and a smiling bland face, she crossed over, to pass the usual knot of guides and taxi-drivers always there waiting for clients. The same bland countenance was presented also for the porter at the entrance, and above the sound of voices, the bustle of arrivals and departures, the clatter the heels of her new sandals made crossing the vast marble floor dissipated apprehension. What did she care what anyone thought—or knew? She only knew herself that a promise had been made . . . and would be kept.

She put out a hand to the doorknob and felt relief as it opened under her touch. It hadn't been locked, then, when it had been tidied for the night. Her back to the hard wood of the door, she leant a moment, legs trembling, tenseness giving way now she was safe.

She flung back the curtains, allowing the early morning sunshine to flood the room, as with careful

hands she smoothed the grey dress over a hanger.
She wondered if she would ever wear it again.
Quickly she pulled down a blue cotton, much like
the lemon one she had worn last evening. Aware as
she was of the climate that was part of this land,
most clothes she had brought had been made of
cotton. The dress went swiftly over her head, and
she gazed fleetingly at the sandals. They would have
to be worn until she could buy another pair.

A quick comb of her hair a dash of lipstick, and
catching up her handbag she went out, locking the
door behind her.

'Good morning, Alexandra.' Alex was surprised
to find Miss Maitland dressed and sitting out on the
small balcony. 'I thought,' she was continuing, 'I
would enjoy the coolness of the morning out here. I
expect I won't have a lot of time to myself, once we
get started on this business of mine today.'

Looking her over, Alex replied with genuine
warmth, 'But you seem so well, Miss Maitland. No
pain?'

'No . . . well, not much. I'm beginning to suspect
it could be this country, or its climate. It really is a
blessing to feel like this. Oh, I don't pretend I feel
like a ten-mile walk, but still. . . . Come along, we'll
get up to breakfast.' She still took hold of the hand
Alex held out, and with her stick on the other side,
they made their way to the lifts.

They weren't escorted this time by a crimson-
jacketed maître d'hotel to their table by the window,
but by their ankle-gowned waiter of last night.
Sipping her second cup of tea, leisurely awaiting her
companion, Alex gazed out over this city of Cairo
though filtered sunshine turned orange by the chiffon
curtains.

'The lady wishes anything more?' Brought back from her recollections of last night, Alex saw that Miss Maitland had finished and shook her head.

Downstairs in the foyer, waiting for Ali, they watched the world go by. They didn't have a long wait. And for the first time as they drove slowly along, they were in the actual city. Alex gazed through her window, enraptured. Not, of course, that everything wore the appearance of a tourist brochure. It didn't! And she grinned widely, listening to some of the strictures Miss Maitland's caustic tongue was uttering.

'We're not at home, Miss Maitland,' she chided gently once, 'The lower class, the peasants, I expect one would say, are poor, as our own were poor only a hundred years or so ago. Modernisation is coming; the attitude towards women is changing. It might be only slowly, but nevertheless it is changing. And look about you,' Alex's tone changed, going gay, 'at the surroundings they have!' The sky above was a deep cloudless blue, the sun shone golden, shedding warmth and colour. Trees in parks raised their waving fronds against blue infinity, a scene, she thought, the perfection of which would always remain a memory.

At their destination, it could have been into any solicitor's office the world over that they were ushered, and from behind the desk the dark, smooth-complexioned, plump owner of it rose to welcome them. Mr Yusef bowed to Miss Maitland, directing her to a chair. To Alex, he merely nodded casually with a raking glance that took in her appearance.

He probably imagines I'm a lady's maid or poor companion, mused Alex to herself, hiding a grin, and settled down in the background to think her own thoughts.

'We realise, my dear madame,' began Mr Yusef, as smoothly as his complexion appeared, 'that it is a long way for you to come. But your late niece's husband's family thought that everything would be better served for you to come to Egypt.'

'Indeed!' The single harsh word brought the obviously prepared speech to a halt.

'Yes ... well. ... My client employed a Brisbane firm to go into your niece's affairs. Her effects belong to her husband now under our laws. Until this sad occasion we didn't realise how great ... how many were the possessions that belonged to her. Your niece, Norma,' here, he directed a deprecating smile to the figure sitting straight-backed, grim, silent, in front of him, 'gave us no idea. Both she and her husband were satisfied with the monthly stipend they received from you.

'However, things have now changed. Your law may not be in accord with ours regarding husbands' rights, but they do acknowledge children as the natural heirs. That, my dear lady,' Mr Yusef still smiled paternally, but his tone allowed no contradiction of the facts, 'is the reason behind this meeting—to put in train your handing over to our Australian counterpart, moneys and properties, for the forwarding of them to Egypt. Also, there is one other thing, but that we will go into later.'

He sat back, confident, smug. This business was simply a straightforward run-of-the-mill affair, to be concluded as quickly as possible. And to have the management of what he thought would be a great deal of money was evidently giving him a great deal of pleasure.

'Your Australian counterpart,' acid dripped from the words, 'didn't apparently delve too deeply into my father's will.' Alex sat up. She had known Miss Maitland always, and had never heard that brusque, almost brutally harsh tone used before.

'. . . . Your pardon, lady? What would that have to do with my client?' Mr Yusef was jolted, his accent more pronounced.

'You were right if you were informed that all properties—with the exception of my own home—and all stocks and bonds are in both names. Divided equally between my brother and myself.' She grinned a vulture's grin, as he raised a hand, accepting this and still satisfied with his lot.

'But my father was a realist,' resumed that grim figure sitting so upright before the desk. 'Since he knew my brother cared nothing for money, for work, only to enjoy himself, everything was left to my power of attorney. His portion was still to be his, but *I*,' the emphasis on that *I* resounded throughout the room, 'had the say on what should or should not be given to him. And also, I might add, that rule applies equally to his heirs.'

The silence of shock reigned in the room. 'But that condition wouldn't apply now, surely?' Mr Yusef's hand, carrying a clean white handkerchief, scurried upwards to wipe a face that was not so smooth or complacent now. 'The man has been dead for years.'

'It applies. It specially applies to my brother's heirs, my father having had experience of the unwanted difficulties into which he could fall.'

'But that's ridiculous! A grown man doesn't have a woman to run his business. It's unheard-of! And that money, that property, belongs to my client's children.'

The old woman grinned her vulture's grin once more and didn't bother to answer. She didn't need to, thought Alex. She would know her position exactly. The man sitting behind the desk, angry, outraged, had been silly to antagonise her at the start, by the calm assumption of just walking in and taking what appeared to be a lot more money than Alex had thought was at stake.

But then no Egyptian male would ever dream of a woman being given power of attorney over a man's possessions. Suddenly an Egyptian man's image flashed before her vision. Goodness, she couldn't imagine a woman being given charge of *his* possessions!

As the old lady glanced round for her stick and nodded to Alex, Mr Yusef broke into speech. 'No, no . . . don't leave, Miss Maitland. Surely something can be worked out? There are the children, you understand. It's their inheritance. . . .'

Interjecting into the silence she still maintained, he continued, 'You haven't yet seen your great-niece or nephew. Couldn't it be arranged for you to do that?'

'I would be quite happy to take them back to Australia. I will even buy . . .' she altered the word, but she had used it deliberately, Alex knew, 'will even come to some arrangement with their father . . . quite a large arrangement for the signing of them over to me.'

'That cannot. . . .' He stopped. 'It might be arranged about the little girl, she speaks English already. But the new son—Raschid would never give him up.'

A cackling laugh interrupted him. 'We'll see. All right, I'll have a look at them, and if I like the look of the girl, this Yasmin, and they want me to, I'll take her home. We'll leave the discussion about the boy till later.'

'About the assets which belong to them. . . .' Clearly the lawyer wanted to salvage some assurance from this interview.

'My brother's share has to, of course, in the nature of things, come to both children. But when they are eighteen! Most likely, I'll be dead by then,' said this implacable woman who spoke as if she had no intention of ever allowing the grim reaper near her. 'However, I've so tied up everything with lawyers and the family court that there would be no way it could be extricated. Unless, of course, they both came to Australia and were made my wards.

'Now, do you want me to see these children? I have the afternoon free, but I want to start booking my air passage home.'

'Yes. . . .' The affirmative was murmured. Clearly, Mr Yusef was thinking. 'That can't be done this afternoon, I'm afraid,' he then said. 'Raschid lives in Luxor. Look, if we arranged it, would you fly there? It is an easy journey and would be very pleasant. There is the Winter Palace to stay at. It's right on the Nile. . . .' He paused, interrupted. His client had turned to the girl.

'Would you like that, Alexandra?'

Alex grinned. She knew the question wasn't to accommodate her. It was Miss Maitland's malicious way of putting Mr Yusef in his place. From experience, she also knew Miss Maitland to be a generous woman. She hoped she would get the little girl at least. So 'Yes, please,' was all she answered.

'I had already booked a table for lunch. I thought you might enjoy eating in an Egyptian restaurant. Now, as I want to get on to these flights for you to Luxor, will you permit Ali to escort you there until I can come?' Mr Yusef rose as he was speaking to accompany them to the door, but his manner was absent.

## CHAPTER FIVE

It was an Egyptian restaurant, they saw, as Ali helped them from the car, set flush with the footpath, its name flaunted large above them in bold Arabic script. Alex cast an anxious glance at the face beside her, but Miss Maitland had no comment to make, and placing her stick firmly on the one step, walked through the door Ali held open.

Apparently they were expected. They were seated, and drinks in long glasses made their appearance immediately. The place was quite pleasant, dim and cool, and they sipped at what were ice-laden orange drinks.

Hesitatingly, not knowing with Miss Maitland, Alex asked, 'Will you bring the little girl home?'

'I wasn't going to let that smooth-faced robber baron Yusef know, but I came with the intention to use money to get them both. I'm a very rich woman, Alexandra—very rich,' the two words were repeated. 'With nurses and servants, and my big home, they would be no problem. Norma's children belong in Australia. So ... we'll go to this place Luxor. You never know, before we finish bargaining, you might have time to see enough sights to satisfy even you. They might not know it, but they are about to come up against someone tougher than old Yusef. I want those children.

'Hush,' she added 'here comes the robber baron! Not one word about the children. Let him think I'm not particularly interested in them.'

Alex ate, allowing the other's talk to wash over her, lids drooping to hide any expression. When would she see him? A shiver of expectation rippled through her. He had told her she would, and recollecting that face, that demeanour, Alex knew that what he said he would do would be done.

Abruptly, she was jerked out of her reverie by a name mentioned. 'Yes,' Mr Yusef was saying, 'Ali told me he was escorting you. Do you know him well?'

'I know him.' Oh, what a whopper, thought Alex. 'But I would like to know more of him,' Miss Maitland was continuing.

'Wouldn't we all?' It was dryly said. 'Everyone walks warily around the Sheik Kasseem ben Omair. No one asks the Omair their business!'

'But who is he? Is he just an Arab sheik of some desert tribe? I shouldn't imagine such a personage would make a sophisticated city professional like you, for instance, Mr Yusef, walk warily.'

'I have had no actual dealings with them.' Stiffly, the words came from their host. 'But I repeat, their business is their business. One also steps out of the way of bodyguards accompanying any of their rulers. They see no one in their path.

'This one you were asking about, the young Kasseem ben Omair, is rumoured to be working in

the far desert. Whatever it entails is given every en-
couragement from the President down. And it also,
I might inform you, is talked about by no one.'

'Surely these days, with the media poking into
everything, there's little that can be kept secret?'

The lawyer's laugh had an edge to it. 'Not even
the most intrepid reporter would try to penetrate
the territory of the Sheik ben Omair! Tribesmen
would shoot first and ask questions afterwards.'

'No one shoots first and asks questions afterwards
nowadays—that's just a cliché. Egypt is not a banana
republic.'

'But the far desert is for the most part Omair territory. They are an extremely wealthy and powerful
tribe, and run their affairs as they see fit. Did you
know,' even with no one in hearing distance around
them, Mr Yusef's voice had dropped to a murmur,
'that this young Sheikh Kasseem is only a quarter
Arab?'

'I did not!' Miss Maitland interjected sharply, and
Alex sat straighter.

'It's no secret, or I wouldn't be mentioning it.
Everyone knows. His grandfather came here between
the two big wars, and like 'El Aurens,' fell in love
with the country. He wandered into Omair territory
and married one of the daughters of the ruling
Sheikh. He never left there again, not even to come
into the city. His son Ahmed was sent to England to
become an engineer like his father.' The lawyer
stopped, glancing at his watch as if deciding to finish
the saga, but the interest of Miss Maitland urged
him on, albeit more reluctantly. 'He married an
Englishwoman. It was known that she disliked this
country, that she hated the desert – even Luxor, and
after this son Kasseem was born, she disappeared.

Some say she went home to England, some say . . . it is not known

'Ahmed ben Omair remarried, a Saudi-Arabian noblewoman. He also doesn't like the desert. He has a place in Luxor, a palace, I'm told. He is also reputed to be wealthy beyond dreams.'

Alex wanted to ask a dozen questions, but policy kept her silent. This Egyptian would reply to Miss Maitland, but he would look on any queries from her as beneath his dignity to answer.

'So this man, Kasseem ben Omair, the one who was with me at the airport——' You're clever, thought Alex, manipulating your words as if he was an acquaintance, without actually saying so; and listened with her ironic smile unnoticed, as her companion continued, ' is actually three-quarters English. He doesn't look it. And he certainly doesn't act it!'

'Oh yes,' again Mr Yusef laughed. 'Both his grandfather and his mother were English. However, he himself is more Arab than the purest blood Egyptian. Egypt and its wellbeing are all he cares about. That, also, is known everywhere. Where his father shuns the desert, preferring the civilisation of Luxor, the son spends all his time there, coming to Cairo only when business makes it necessary.'

Mr Yusef bent his head to a waiter speaking quietly in his ear. 'I must go, my dear lady—I have a phone call. Ali is with the car outside. Why don't you allow him to take you round the bazaar? He nodded and walked hurriedly away.

'I expect we may as well,' said Miss Maitland. 'I want to take home a few souvenirs. And as we have the afternoon free, we may as well shop.'

'The lady is pleased?' Ali had escorted them to the

lift and was handing over packages to the porter.

'Yes, thank you, Ali. We'll see you tomorrow.' Miss Maitland's weight was more heavily on Alex's arm than when they had left the hotel this morning. But it had been a long day and it was evening now.

'Are we really going to Luxor tomorrow? asked Alex, as they both dropped on to the older woman's bed. 'And are you pleased with the outcome of today's business?'

'Yes, we're certainly going to this damn place Luxor, tomorrow, and yes again, if not pleased, I'm satisfied.'

Gazing at that old face, at the grin of almost malignancy it was cheerfully showing, Alex laughed. 'You're a wicked old witch, you know that, I suppose.' But she held up a wrist—not the one with the white impression that a missing wrist watch had left behind on a brown arm—and looked admiringly at the one from which dropped a chain bracelet of gold, with its one exquisite charm of Nefertiti. It was a present that that witch-like old woman had insisted upon buying for her, brushing aside Alex's quite genuine protests.

'Shall I pack these away,' she asked, indicating the four or five packages lying there, 'in your over-night case?'

'Oh, I expect so—anywhere. I'm tired, Alexandra. Run me a bath.'

Alex glanced swiftly around. Her companion did indeed look tired. She set about the task of collecting paraphernalia, and turning down the bed.

On her way into the dining room, Alex gave the order for Miss Maitland's dinner to be sent down, ate the one course she had ordered for herself, drank her coffee, then made her way through the ante-room on to the big patio with its tables and chairs, high above the city.

She stood at the railings gazing out and over it, recollections of so many impressions crowding her memory. Of course, there was the one overriding one. But that he was mostly English had to be taken in too. With Kasseem, she hadn't thought or cared about his nationality. She did, however, feel on safer ground knowing he was partly English.

Smiling absently at a couple who sat near them in the dining room, and who had also sauntered out to look over the river and the city lights, she answered their goodnights and went back to her dreaming.

No notice at all was taken as glass doors swung open and a presence came to stand beside her. Irritable at the nearness when there was uncrowded empty space all around, she moved away.

Footsteps followed her footsteps, and a voice above said, 'There was another occasion when you didn't take flight from my vicinity.'

'Kasseem!' It was a whisper, and her body swung to meet his, so close.

The gleam of white showed in the dark bronze of his face—a face that she hardly knew. Brown hair—not the ebony black she had thought it would be, went skittering through a mind in turmoil—crowned a countenance exposed entirely by the absence of the familiar kaffiyeh. However, there was one thing that hadn't changed. His lids still drooped half-shut, hiding all thoughts and · expression behind them.

Alex's glance raked swiftly over him in his Western suit, then back to meet the ironical gaze' being bestowed upon her. 'I didn't need to tell you my name, it seems. But then I know how gossip travels in Egypt. It also tells me, however, that you are flying to Luxor tomorrow.'

'Yes . . . yes, we are. But how on earth could you know that? It was only settled about lunch-time. . . .'

An eyebrow went up. 'As I have just been inform-ing you, gossip runs like a fire in the East.'

'You said I'd see you. . . . I didn't know when. . . .' She was stammering. She stopped, in an endeavour to make her words sound more coherent. 'I don't know how long we'll be in Luxor. Please, shall I see you when I come back?'

'I don't expect to be in Cairo.' It was his turn to pause as his gaze took in the distress showing so openly on the expressive face just below his. But his hand went out sharply to hold her away, as her body arched more closely to meet his.

'Good God, Alexandra! This is a public place. Do you think I want gossip to run riot even more than it's probably doing now? You will have to realize that here nothing, no little thing, goes unnoticed.'

'I don't care. . . .'

'But I do!' Both eyebrows went up this time, and green eyes looked directly into hers. 'I said I didn't expect to be in Cairo. I do know I'll be in Luxor. Keep away, for Allah's sake!' The ejaculation was needed. She had taken the pace necessary to fit into the curves of his body.

Obediently, Alex complied with that violent sen-tence. Now they could have been merely ordinary acquaintances passing a few minutes in idle con-versation. 'All right, I will! But shall I see you in Luxor?'

He was laughing, shoulders shaking with silent mirth. 'Do you know, Alexandra,' he said softly, 'this situation between us is too absurd. It should be I, the wicked sheikh, making all the advances, and you, the shrinking maiden, using every endeavour to hold me at bay. I'll tell you this, though. If you don't watch out you'll push your luck too far one of these days.'

'Again, I don't care. But, Kasseem, it's all right for you. You can make, or not make, us to meet. You must know I . . . that I don't want to leave Egypt, leave you. . . . That to go home to Australia and live my life out will be dust and ashes. . . .' She couldn't go on. Fancy saying such words to him!

Into the silence between them, she asked again, the thought of not ever seeing him colouring her tone with entreaty, 'Shall I see you in Luxor?'

Laughter had been wiped clean from his face. 'All right, Alexandra. I'll be busy, more than just busy, I expect, with important visitors. But yes, I'll manage it somehow. . . . And, Alexandra . . .' he repeated her name, this time gravely, 'I know how you feel. How could I help it? But I don't want this attraction to end in tragedy. It might be best for you to go home to Australia without any meeting in Luxor. I know the misery that can arise out of the merging of different cultures. And another thing,' here, the tone went inflexible, 'I might find myself with commitments I could have to honour.'

'I don't care about any of that. It's in the future.' Her tone held as much inflexibility as his had done.

'Very well, then. Give me five minutes before you come inside.' He reached for her hand and dropped into it a twisted scrap of tissue, closing it firmly. She didn't even glance down, only looked at the face opposite.

Without another word he turned and walked away. Alex stood gazing out over the city, the noise

of which reached her, even this far up. Hearing and
seeing nothing, the minutes counted away, she
pushed open the doors and marched through the
crowded ante-room as if it were empty.

In her room, she dropped into a chair. Finding
her fingers tight clenched, hurting, she glanced down
at them. Unwrapped, the twist of paper disclosed a
watch.

Lips twisted. Of course! Like the dress and sandals,
this also could have belonged to her, except that it
was no mass-produced working piece such as hers
had been. What did she care for exquisite watches
or original dresses! What did she care about different
cultures, either—if you acknowledged they were there.

Drawing a deep breath, she clasped the watch
over the white bare patch, which it covered almost
exactly. Her lips twisted again, thinking of the de-
liberation that must have been expended on the
purchase of it. On her other hand the profile of
Nefertiti looked up at her. 'I'm not beautiful as you
were, or even high-born like Mustafa's "my lord",'
she murmured, 'but we'll see.'

Short work was made of preparing for bed, but it
was long hours before the borderland of sleep came
to claim her.

It could have been a mere thread of cotton winding
through the brownness entirely surrounding it. When
you came to think of it, thought Alex, although one
treated clichés with disdain, they must have origi-
nated from somewhere. Because from way up here
in the sky, the Nile showed the merest sliver of width
with a smudge on both sides indicating the growth
of green. Also showing was the occasional bulge
denoting a town or village. Flying over the place,

one actually saw the immensity of the desert, and that it certainly lived up to its name. Suddenly she saw lines spoking out from one of the bulges and what looked like vehicles moving as slowly as caterpillars upon it. Probably an army convoy from the looks of it, went through her mind. She grinned. There was that shadow again. On and off, the shade of their plane had fled before them upon the sand far below like an escort never caught up with, or, as they turned, it was following, a reflection incredibly real.

Startled, so fascinated by the antics of the shadow plane, she turned as the hostess touched her. 'We'll be in Luxor in a few minutes. Fasten your seat-belts, please.'

It was less than the few minutes mentioned when the bump of touchdown came. Collecting both overnight bags, Alex slung her own from her shoulder, walking down the small corridor behind Miss Maitland with the other. They didn't have far to walk; it had been only a tiny plane in which they had flown.

'Good heavens!'

'What is it?' Almost alarmed at that tone, Alex stepped swiftly out on to the steps. The airport, as their plane had been, was small, like a country stop at home, nothing at all like the crowded, strident one of Cairo.

'It's the heat!' Miss Maitland was complaining as they stepped down to begin the walk to the low cement structure that was the terminal.

'Oh, come on, Miss Maitland. We've experienced worse scorchers at home in Brisbane in summer time. It's a beautiful day. Just think what it would be like if it was raining!'

'We might have it hot at home in the summer,

but there are only occasional days like that. Here it's hot all the time. Anyway, I'm allowed to grumble if I want to!'

A swift glance at the old face showed not malicious mischief today, but a sense of strain. She was too old for all this gallivanting around, thought Alex almost angrily. 'Look, come on, love,' she was saying, and did not know that she had used the term of endearment to the awe-inspiring woman whom she, as well as most of the other girls in the library, had always treated with circumspection, 'we'll soon be in the cool, and have a cup of tea as soon as we get to the hotel.'

'I hope there's someone to meet us,' the irritable voice still continued. 'I don't want a repeat of the Cairo fiasco.'

Heavens, how I wish we could! went through Alex's mind. But of course, Kasseem wouldn't be in Luxor today. He had been left behind in Cairo. But he would come. He had said so!

And it wasn't the tall, aloof, arrogant figure of Kasseem who stepped out to meet them, although it was an Egyptian. Older, and of only average height, he walked towards them unhesitatingly.

'Aunt Elizabeth!' He held out a hand.

'Raschid?'

He looks nice, was Alex's first thought. And then, But he also looks apprehensive. He wasn't handsome or in any way outstanding. Dark smooth complexion surrounded large brown eyes that held a worried expression.

He doesn't look like a man interested in selling a daughter for money, was Alex's next thought, and she smiled at him as he was introduced.

'Yes, I recognise you—Alex, isn't it? Your likeness

is among a lot of snaps Norma . . . my wife had. She liked to take them out and look at them.' He said suddenly, as if not meaning to, 'I miss her. . . . I can't believe it has happened.' For a moment he was silent, his back turned, then he continued gently, 'I have a car waiting to take you to the hotel.'

Lying back in her corner of the car on the long journey into Luxor, Alex allowed the conversation of the other two to wash over her. The road drove a wedge through a jungle of green on both sides. For mile after uncounted mile, vegetable fields were being tended, date palms grew tall against a sky of the deepest azure. The warmth of gold and blue always surrounding the senses here in the desert country would be the memory one would take home of Egypt. Suddenly, catching at her vision, three immense palms rose to the heavens. Whether it was the way that their fronds caught a slice of infinity between the lacy spread of leaves, she didn't know. But held there was a piece of incredible colour, indigo mixed with lapis lazuli, so intense, so breath-taking, she strained to hold it to her. Turning, as the car swept past, she saw it was gone; the small vignette of beauty had disappeared. Only the date palms and a sky of ordinary blue met her vision.

'Here we are,' Raschid was saying, as they ran along a road with buildings on one side, the river on the other. Before an ediface coloured bright lollipop-pink, stretching far back in its single story, they stopped.

Anxiously, Raschid glanced at his wife's aunt. 'It is the old Winter Palace Hotel that the British used for holidays at Luxor. The new one, look, is next door. Mr Yusef thought you might rather stay in this one, but we can easily change your bookings.'

'Oh no! The exclamation came from Alex, who then put up an involuntary hand as if to silence the words.

'Of course not, Raschid,' Miss Maitland was answering dryly. 'You surely couldn't imagine we would prefer to go to a new, air-conditioned, luxury tourist hotel like that one, would you?' indicating the immense multi-story, modern hotel rising to the heavens. 'Especially when we can live in a romantic pink sugar-cake like this one in front of us. What would you say, Alexandra?'

Knowing she was being got at, Alex replied only, 'One can stay in tourist hotels like that all over the world. This one has an air all of its own.'

'It is comfortable inside. You will like it.' Apparently not understanding the play of words between the two women, Raschid looked anxious.

'I'm sure we shall, Raschid,' Alex told him as they mounted the few steps to the divided landing, and then up into the hotel; the ubiquitous porters following with the luggage.

Taking their passports to the desk, Raschid returned, saying he had ordered tea.

For the first time on this long day, Miss Maitland appeared to relax and smile naturally. 'Thank you, Raschid—just what I need. There is one good thing about Egypt, one can always get a cup of tea. Maybe another legacy from when the British were here.'

'I expect tea was drunk a lot then, but I took it in England when I was studying there,' Raschid told her. 'And Norma . . .' a hesitation sounded, 'we drank it together all the time.'

He's nice, and what's more, he's kind too, thought Alex. She rose, wanting to leave them alone to talk, saying, 'I'll go and settle us in, Miss Maitland.'

She liked the big old-fashioned room, with its large ceiling fan that they had given to the older woman. No balcony was here. On the ground floor, the windows looked out over gardens. She followed her own case to a room farther along the corridor, and grinned as she looked around.

Probably Mr Yusef's idea of what was her due, she decided, almost laughing. It was small, but had its own bathroom, and it would suit her very well.

Taking the cup of tea her could-be employer poured and handed to her, she drank it, ate a cake from the dish, and heard the plans for tomorrow.

'I've been invited to Raschid's home, Alexandra, to meet his family—and my great-niece and nephew. Not expecting anyone with me, the invitation doesn't include you. No . . . no . . .!' She held up a restraining hand as Raschid began to protest that certainly Alex should come along too. 'There are enough temples and ruins to keep her occupied, and as we hope not to be staying here for long, she had better see as much as she can, instead of sitting round being polite to a houseful of strangers.

'Now, I seem to have been sitting down all day. I think I would like a little walk, maybe to look at a few shops, and have a closer look at this famous Nile of Alex's. It is quite in order to walk about here in safety, isn't it, Raschid? That was something we were warned not to do in the middle of Cairo without a guide. But this looks more like a country village than a city.'

Goodness, if she knew about my little episode in Cairo, I wonder what she'd think—and say to me? wondered Alex, only half listening to Raschid's reply. 'Yes, of course. There are plenty of tourists here in Luxor all the time, winter and summer. It is kept very law-abiding. You might be bothered by touts attempting to sell you souvenirs, but just be firm, and they'll leave you alone. And yes, you will find it pleasing to walk by the river now, the sun is getting low. Aunt Elizabeth!' He took her hand, smiled at Alex, and departed.

They strolled from their pink iced-cake hotel and found an arcade just beyond the new Winter Palace. Even Miss Maitland was impressed at the carvings, the silver and gold, the ornaments and jewellery being displayed. 'I'll come back here before we leave, Alexandra,' she said. 'It will be less distracting to shop here than in the bazaars at Cairo. Come along now, we'll walk by the river for a while. It should be cool there with the breeze off the water.'

## CHAPTER SIX

SLOWLY beside the water of the Nile, they strolled, and it was cool as Raschid had promised. Palm trees provided the shade, and a breeze from across the water the coolness, as it wafted over them as they walked. Abruptly, shattering the idle scene about them, there was movement, hurried, even frenzied. Egyptians in long coffee-coloured gowns, souvenir touts, youths always present at any hour—even the knot of guides and dragomen in front of the two hotels were hurrying off the roadway, down behind the wall that guarded the river, up to press close against the façade of the hotel front. Even the drivers of the buggies clip-clopping leisurely on the lookout for passengers whipped up their horses and disappeared in a flurry of racing hooves down side streets. And all around the murmuring noise of quick-spoken Arabic sounded.

Astonished, the two women stood there wondering what all the frenzied commotion was about. However, coming to them, the sound of horses being ridden quite fast echoed along the empty street. Alex eased Miss Maitland up behind a palm tree against the stone wall.

Then she saw them. A troop of horses were cantering along, stretching across the whole road. Still some distance away, Alex saw they would come too close. She took a step in front of the old woman, and was determinedly pushed aside.

'No, you don't, Alexandra. I want to see this too.'

Dressed in white, on beautiful, splendid horses, they seemed fierce, wild men, and the guns slung across their shoulders did nothing to dispel this impression.

'Heavens!' muttered Alex, her gaze on the one who rode in front. Also in white, this one had the addition of a black burnous trimmed with silver hanging loose, and a kaffiyeh bound with the same black and silver cord that she remembered. Young, breathtaking, he was a part of the black stallion he bestrode, and he was arrogance personified.

A few yards to the front he cantered, four horsemen grouped closely about him. These were young men too, clean-shaven, riding with the same arrogant certainty that theirs was the right of way, anywhere, any time. The rest of the troop were older, bearded, carrying however the same assumption of omnipotence. In an easy canter the whole cortège was up and past them, and from all around, though spoken in Arabic, the words ben Omair echoed in exclamations and excited chatter. Even so, Alex noticed that though the horsemen were long past, voices were kept low and spoken only among themselves.

'Well . . .!' Caustic, acidic, was the tone in which Miss Maitland spoke. 'Now I can really imagine the Middle Ages! That little exhibition could have been one of the Henrys making a triumphal entry into a captured city, with serfs and peasants scuttling before them. I didn't expect that in this day and age such a spectacle could happen.

Alex laughed. 'But then you're prejudiced against this country. It was showmanship, I admit. No one was hurt; no one was at a disadvantage. And it was something to have seen, now wasn't it?'

'For someone young and romantic, I expect it could be. For me, I'm going back to the hotel where civilisation has caught up to the present day.'

They had dinner in a garden surrounded by plants and trees. There was no moon, but stars hung huge and brilliant from a black velvet canopy. Softened by a meal that was superb and chosen by an attentive waiter, it was in harmony that they rose and made their way to the hotel proper. It was early to bed for both of them; the older woman to plot and plan concerning her niece and nephew, Alex to pull a pillow over her head, and think of a man she would be seeing . . . some time, here in this ancient city of Luxor.

'Alexandra,' said Miss Maitland the next morning, as they sat in the lounge after a late breakfast.

'Yes?' Alex glanced up from the book in her lap that she was supposed to be reading.

'This letter from Raschid has just been delivered

to me. After apologising again that owing to family commitments, you'll be here alone, he goes on to say there's something called "Sound and Light" being staged at the Karnak temple tonight. He says you will enjoy it and that the hotel will provide you with a dragoman—again, whatever that may mean. I guess,' here she gave the young girl that malicious grin of hers when amused, 'you won't dislike too much the idea of putting in your time at such a spectacle.'

Alex grinned back, and there was no sign of maliciousness in this smile. 'How nice of Raschid,' she answered. 'And of course you know I would love it. I'll arrange it at the desk. Now, how do you feel about Norma's children when it's getting so close to seeing them? You know, Miss Maitland, I like Raschid,' she added. 'He's not putting on any act for you. You've said Norma's letters showed her love. I think Raschid loved her very much too. All that expectation of a lot of money Mr Yusef showed so blatantly may come from his family, not from Raschid himself. He's a younger son, you say.'

'Yes.' The older woman heaved a sigh. 'I actually like him too. Alexandra, and I didn't mean to. And the money will have to go at some stage. I'm only seeking to do what's best for Norma's children.'

They spent an easy morning, Miss Maitland, tired but in no pain, resting. Alex went wandering, but always within seeing distance of the hotel. She stood by the river, watching its traffic. No one bothered her, no one slid souvenirs into her face. In fact there was empty space always about her. Raschid arrived, and Miss Maitland was whisked away.

Alex decided to read until it was time to dress for the Karnak Temple show. Only an hour or so

remained to be put in as it was a before-dinner affair.
She sat by her small window, a book in her lap, and
as this morning also, her eyes took in none of the
printed sentences. Her thoughts overrode any
engraved words.

A knock upon the door brought her head round.
She had heard no sound of arrival. Frowning a little,
she walked across to open it. Mustafa stood there.
He proffered a sealed letter. 'My lord said to read it;
that everything is arranged.' He bowed and went
away before Alex could reply or thank him.

Her back to the wooden door she had closed, Alex
looked the missive over. A thick cream envelope with
Arabic script in one corner met her gaze, and in
flowing letters right across the width of it her name
had been inscribed. This must be Kasseem's writing,
she thought, gazing at the firm, bold letters.

Unable to make herself tear open the envelope,
she retrieved a nail file from her handbag and slit
carefully beneath the flap.

> I keep my word, you see, however difficult it
> may be to do so. Mustafa will collect you at six. I
> am sure that having some acquaintance of you, to
> take you anywhere but to the Sound and Light
> exhibition being staged at Karnak tonight would
> amount to almost sacrilege.
>
> > In haste,
> > Kasseem.

Alex read it through a second time, then stared at
the signature. Kasseem! How like him. No saluta-
tions, no hint of affection. But his word had been
kept. She wondered how he had got down to Luxor.
There wouldn't have been time for a boat to arrive—
then she remembered a helicopter flying low an hour

or so ago while she had been in the garden. A glance at Kasseem's present showed her it was after five o'clock, and no thought at all came of wondering what to wear. She knew!

More lavish than usual with skin perfume and talcum, she came from the bathroom and donned all the clothes her escort of tonight had brought for her, adding only pink side-combs that almost matched the cyclamen edging of her grey dress to her brushed and shining hair.

She was nervous, she knew, trying to subdue the butterflies fluttering away under her diaphragm, making her hands shake. It's silly, she thought, to feel like this. I acknowledge that some excited expectation is in order, but to feel as if tonight is the beginning and end of the world is too ridiculous. I know him! This is no alarming stranger I'm meeting. She wished the few moments of waiting would pass, because her nervousness was increasing, not departing. Still, she almost jumped as the expected knock came upon her door.

She opened it to greet Mustafa—and found the butterflies jumping everywhere. She looked her escort over in silence—at the pants that fitted as they did a model from the glossy magazines; the white roll-top cashmere sweater which did duty for a shirt. At hair brushed in Western style; at the dark, bronzed, aloof aquiline countenance.

'Normally, I can tell what you are thinking, Alexandra, with that expressive face of yours. However, just now you've lost me. What is it that brings that look into your eyes?'

A moment more she gazed at him, then she spoke slowly as if the words came of their own accord. 'I was just wishing that for once in my life, for this one night, I could be glamorous, exotic, beautiful! Instead of——' she threw out an arm in a throw-away gesture, 'oh, I know I'm reasonably attractive, I have eyebrows that lift my face a little out of the ordinary. I also have a figure that could be called better than average, but. . . .' Her words trailed away.

An eyebrow went up above those green eyes, and the face smiled, a white gleam in the bronze. The first time, she realised, she had seem him actually smile. She had heard that silent laughter upon the roof-garden of Shepheards Hotel when he had men-tioned innocent maidens and wicked sheikhs. But this was genuine amusement.

'Dare I tell you,' he was saying, and the words came softly, 'that I have ... shall I say, been involved with women who were—what were your words?—glamorous, exotic, beautiful, and even more descriptive adjectives that could have been applied. And I could leave them all without one regret. I am not saying, you understand, that they did not attract me at the time, but they were surface affairs, and were left behind when the time came without one backward glance. Does that tell you anything, Alexandra, because if you knew the stratagems I have had to resort to to get this one night to myself, you would stop uselessly wishing you were anyone but who you are. Come! I wouldn't want you to be late for this spectacle you are going to delight in ... but before we go, am I allowed to congratulate you on that creation you are wearing? Did you choose it just to wear for me tonight?'

'Do you know, Kasseem,' that flying ebony arch that was her own eyebrow rose as far as it could be made to do so, 'some man bought it for me, and

everything else that I'm wearing for you tonight. Do
you imagine he might want payment for it—in kind,
I mean?'

This time he laughed out loud. 'You never know.
Should I warn you to be careful of him? Especially
at being alone with him . . . in bedrooms of launches,
for instance.' His teasing smile took in her expectant
face, and abruptly he reached behind her to pull
shut the door. He stood aside allowing her to precede
him. He didn't take her arm. He never did touch
her, she realised, except. . . .

Through the hallway, into and across the big
lounge, they walked. Alex looked neither to right or
left, yet knowing they were the cynosure of all eyes—
the Western ones admiring her escort; the staff, who
didn't even look their way, but who knew every
movement the man beside her made—and she
wondered why he had come to collect her himself,
instead of sending Mustafa.

Down the few steps on the divided stairway, then
into the large black car resting almost on the footpath, through the open door of the back seat she
went, to have the body of Kasseem drop down beside
her. The chauffeur, in Western dress, closed the door.
Alex glanced at the other two men in native costume
who filled the rest of the space in the front seat and
wondered. Next to her a sharp sentence in Arabic
erupted. One of the Arabs turned, and with hand to
forehead, lips and heart, replied when he had
finished his obeisance. His tone, while sounding con-
ciliatory, yet held a determination that was un-
mistakable.

Kasseem leaned forward and pressed buttons, and
the opaque side windows slid open, the glass partition between the two seats going upwards with a

rush. Alex saw the beginning of a smile curl the firmness of her companion's lips.

His hand had dropped down on to the seat between them, and her fingers stole to rest against it. Not touching; with all her determined insistence on obtaining his promise to see her again, using physical proximity in regard to Kasseem was unthinkable.

But her hand was taken and hard fingers entwined wth hers. The hands lay upon the seat, laced together, sending the throb of pulses soaring. Happiness is this! It is now! It wasn't coherent, the thought that trembled through her mind, Alex knew, but whatever came in the future, riding down this broad thoroughfare to Karnak was a memory that would last her life through.

She spoke softly, almost a little shyly. 'They look like some men I saw yesterday riding along here.' Her glance rested upon the two bearded, fierce-looking men seated in the front seat.

'They probably are those men. And I'm afraid you are going to have to put up with them being around the whole night. We are expecting important visitors tomorrow, and as the government saw fit to send down almost half the damned army as security for them, my uncle decided that the honour of the Omair deserved no less. Hence an escort had to be dispatched for one of their own. And that one, I'll have you know, is me!' A burst of Arabic escaped him then, and Alex wondered if that was how swearing in Arabic sounded.

'But surely you wouldn't need protection, Kasseem?' she queried. 'Especially down here where you're known, where your father lives?'

'Of course I don't, Alexandra. No one would dare touch one of us—my uncle knows that! But he thinks that even princes are not as important as any Sheikh of the Omair tribe. In many other things he can be made to listen to reason, but the dignity and the prestige of our tribe, as far as he is concerned, is sacrosanct.'

'You should have heard Miss Maitland's strictures upon them as they rode past.' Alex gave a little giggle as she remembered. 'But heavens, Kasseem, that young man who rode in front acted like a Sultan of Baghdad would behave, way back in the Middle Ages!'

The man beside her, holding her hand, laughed— for the second time that night. 'Ahmed—yes, I expect he did. It was an honour for him to be sent. And I might tell you he wasn't acting, however it looked. That's the way he lives. He'll have to calm down some before he becomes the paramount Sheikh. But the way he behaves, and for that matter, the way all the tribesmen act, is the reason for the reputation the Omair have. However,' the strong shoulders went up in a shrug, 'civilisation is creeping closer, and with all their wealth and power, and they are very wealthy and very powerful, maybe it will put a brake on young Ahmed.

'Would you like to hear his description of you, Alexandra?' he asked.

'Description of me? How could he describe me? He's never seen me, never set eyes on me.'

'Oh, yes, yes he has seen you. He saw you yesterday when he was riding through to my father's house.'

'Yesterday? He didn't see anyone. Even if a poor native had fallen beneath his horse's hooves, he wouldn't have seen him. He would have ridden right over him.'

'No native would be silly enough to allow himself within falling distance of any Omair horseman.'

'But, Kasseem, even if he had seen Miss Maitland and myself, he wouldn't have known who we were. Also, we were up against the river wall, well out of the way.'

'Take it from me, he saw you—and he knew who you were.'

'Kasseem——' She drew both entwined hands up, and leant her cheek against the outside dark one. 'Kasseem,' she repeated, 'what does that mean? That they know that I . . . that you. . . .'

'Oh, didn't I tell you? I thought I mentioned it in Cairo. Everything is noted in the East. And if you thought for one moment, Alexandra, that I could have a woman on my launch for an entire night, and not have it reported to both my father and my uncle, you have another think coming, to use English slang. Not that such an event, I might inform you, would worry either of them in the slightest. But to them both I am important; I belong to the Omair tribe, and so have a guard upon me, always. Now, do you want to hear what my young cousin Ahmed thought of you?'

'No, I don't! I'm beginning to feel like a guinea pig in a cage, with everyone looking in,' Alex complained.

'Oh, I expect there'll be times when you won't be on display, that I guarantee. And one of those times might be later tonight. After this Sound and Light, would you like to have dinner wth me back on the launch?'

'Oh, yes, please! Is the launch here? I thought there wouldn't be time for it to sail here by now.'

'It left before either of us did. I came to Luxor in

a helicopter. Look! You're being waved at.'

Startled by the abrupt change of topic, Alex glanced out of her side window, even while thinking he was like his cousin Ahmed, being aware of events transpiring around him when seemingly totally engrossed in his own affairs. A whole stream of carriages were clip-clopping sedately along the wide road. From one that they were passing at this moment, a woman waved gaily, and a drawl that could only originate in the south of the U.S.A. called across to them.

A busload of American tourists were staying at the hotel, and Alex had had conversations with this particular woman a number of times. She returned the gay wave smilingly and leaned forward to call back a greeting, and then their vehicle had drawn ahead. She had used her unoccupied hand, however. She hadn't freed the one where she wanted it to remain.

The car pulled up in a large open-air park in which all sorts of vehicles were already scattered about—carriages with their drivers attending to the horses belonging to them, cars, both small and large, besides one big tourist bus. Their own back door was opened first on Kasseem's side, and he leaned back inside to help her to alight. Alex looked, bemused, at the mighty bulk of the temple beyond this busy place, where ankle-robed natives talked and laughed, apparently not troubled at all or caring that this vast edifice of their ancestors had seen the seasons of almost four thousand years come and go about it. She wondered suddenly with a little shiver if the shades of those long-departed inhabitants still occupied this place.

'Are you all right? Surely you can't be cold?'

Kasseem was looking down at her, puzzled.

She moved closer to him, saying, half laughing, half seriously, 'No, I'm not cold—how could I be? I was just wondering if any spirits of the departed dead, men who actually had the expertise to erect and build such a monument, were reluctant to leave it.'

'Shame on you, Alexandra!' Kasseem was laughing his silent laugh, shoulders shaking. 'And you possessing not one drop of blood belonging to the mystic East! Now, I've been through the place times without number, and no spirits have ever haunted me. Still, come along, we'll go and find out if it's different tonight.'

Past the entrance between the double row of small statues that could have been either human or animal, the crowd began to wend, hearing the words of the temple guide beginning the story of the place as it was in the beginning. As the beautiful voice, English, probably Shakespearean trained by the sound of it, echoed all about them, Alex gazed around. There were no visible loudspeakers, and she wondered at the expertise that allowed that voice to be heard with equal clarity wherever one moved.

As they emerged into what seemed a courtyard, a blaze of light was suddenly bathing them in brilliance. Against the base of a column that rose to the very sky and clearly had been one of the supports of this incredible place of worship, Alex trailed her hand, feeling its rough sandstony composition. How could these mighty columns have possibly been constructed in that primitive era that was the beginning of time as they knew it?

Turning impulsively to Kasseem, she saw that he was already looking at her, an eyebrow raised, an

almost lopsided smile on his face. 'Don't tell me,
Alexandra; don't even begin to ask me, either, as I
know you had every intention of doing. Of course I
think the conception, never mind the building of this
temple, was a triumph of some master-mind. I look
at it with pride as an inheritance reaching back
through the ages. But I am not a romantic like you.
It is the modern world of today we have all got to
live in. My own ambition is a better life for ordinary
people; not to erect a vast, soaring edifice like this to
some gods. So come along and dream your dreams
while this voice from infinity tells you all about it.'

'You're a Philistine, Kasseem. I wouldn't have
believed it!' she told him, but she came along, and
the night dissolved into brilliance in one part of the
ruins, ebony night in another, with that perfect voice
from the heavens always beckoning them on, until
finally they found themselves seated in a kind of
grandstand above the temple which had certainly
been built by no ancient hand.

'Look!' The whisper came from Kasseem, close
against her from necessity in the crush of seating, the
two Arab men of the Omair tribe immediately behind.
Softly, from some distant position, the light was
pinpointing the statue of a woman standing tall, her
face in profile, displaying perfection. Alex touched
the little gold charm on her bracelet, asking, 'Is it
Nefertiti? It's as beautiful as she was reputed to be.'

'Not in this temple, I'm afraid, my little romantic.'
There was a laugh in the soft reply. 'Look,' he told
her again, indicating a region in the opposite direction.

Alex's gaze followed the pointing finger. Away in
the desert, a very long away, she would have
thought, the faintest of light was becoming visible,

turning from the palest green to pulsating emerald. Out of nowhere, an oasis was rising, date palms standing tall, etching their fronds against a night sky, the usual jungle of green nestling about their base.

'How is it done? It's incredible! One would imagine it was there, standing in daylight, and that one could walk into it.' Her words were also spoken in a whisper, and she reached for Kasseem's hand, uncaring if the two Arabs behind saw or not.

'Oh, we moderns have some expertise too,' again a laugh was in his voice. 'Electricity, and the use of lights and stage effects can also bring that look to your face, I see, as well as ancient temples constructed almost four thousand years ago. Still, I think both the ancient and the new give pleasure to our visitors, and today that is the main thing. However, Alexandra, this is almost the end of the show. I don't want to get caught in this crowd for an hour or so on the way out, so we'll leave now. Come along.' Her arm was taken and they sidestepped down from the forms.

They left behind a rising swell of music, and the last of that voice from on high's message. With one of the Omair striding along in front now, because they were picking their way through the unoccupied ruins of the temple, and the other behind them, it still took some time to reach the car park.

And it was a noisy place into which they debouched—carriage drivers calling out, guides and dragomen rushing to greet early returning tourists. No one, Alex noted again, came near their vicinity. They could have been walking through a deserted, empty square.

The car travelled more swiftly on its return journey than the leisurely sightseeing passage they had enjoyed going to Karnak; and silence reigned in its interior. Kasseem leaned back, eyes half shut, while Alex, unwilling to waste one moment of this exceptional night, gazed through her window, at the buildings and other temples on one side, at the gleam of water visible between the cultivated trees and the ubiquitous date palms on the other. Always, she knew, the sight of any kind of palms etched against the heavens would bring back memories of Egypt, and the bonus Egypt had given to her ... Kasseem.

He was speaking now in Arabic, the glass partition lowered. He was answered in the same language. Then they were stopping, and out of the car window Alex saw the so familiar outline of the launch that she had last seen tied up to a jetty on the Nile at Cairo.

It seemed their bodyguard wasn't coming aboard. Only Mustafa was there to greet them as they trod the small gangplank to its deck. Alex heaved a sigh. Would she ever compress the kaleidoscopic sights and sounds of these last few hours into a manageable size for her memory bank? And then she realised, as an engine burst into sound and the launch began moving to midstream, that this night wasn't yet over.

## CHAPTER SEVEN

KASSEEM'S hand made an arch in the empty air towards the bow of the launch, and obediently Alex preceded him in that direction. They stood leaning upon the rail, watching the wash of the ship's wake streaming back on both sides. Alex's gaze came upwards, and she saw the river, distant from the disturbance their passage was making, still, calm, reflecting pinpoints of starshine.

From the banks on both sides, occasional lights shone forth, showing that they weren't the only ones not abed. For the length of the journey, until the engine stopped and their conveyance was motionless upon the water beneath them, Kasseem remained silent, and, wondering at this, Alex found herself unable to break it.

Suddenly he moved, not to take her in his arms, as she was half expecting, and, as she admitted honestly to herself, which would be the crowning attribute of the whole night, but to come and stand behind, pulling her against him, curve fitting to curve; his arms coming to meet at her waist. No other attempt at lovemaking ensued.

They remained so, only the occasional sound from the land, and the soft slap of water beneath them, disturbing the night's stillness. Alex lay quiet, eyes closed, her entire weight leaning upon, and being supported by, the long tensile length moulding her body. Then, erupting out of nowhere, another dimension had arrived. Alex felt the tremor that rippled through the figure at her back, and as he moved to gather her more closely, she twisted, her feet on tiptoe, stretching, her arms linked behind his neck, allowing no room for so much as a breeze from the river to separate them.

'Alexandra . . . Alexandra. . . .' The two words came from against her throat, and she wouldn't have recognised that it was Kasseem's voice. For another minute, another eternity, there was no movement, then she was set away, and she heard the jagged breath being expelled.

'Mustafa has prepared dinner, we'll go and see about eating it.' Kasseem propelled her towards the cockpit and then under the canopy.

The table was set, Alex saw; the table which was probably used for charting, for the running of the launch. Folded back against the wall normally, it was now pulled upright and set with damask, silver and glassware. Alex wasn't hungry, she didn't feel like eating. She glanced at the man, who turned when she didn't take the seat he had pulled forward.

'Good God, Alexandra, don't look at me like that! For Allah's sake, allow me at least some leeway in which to manoeuvre. Look—we will eat, and when we are calmer, we'll talk. Do you imagine that I want to just talk? Don't you know that all I want to do is take you downstairs and make love to you? You give me no help, and there are things that have to be said.'

At those words, at that tone, obediently she subsided into the seat. Kasseem lifted lids off dishes and heaped her plate. 'You won't have tasted these birds,' he told her, evidently trying to make normal conversation. 'They are not at all like English game, and are cooked in spices and herbs as they were in ancient times.'

A kind of a giggle escaped Alex, and a hand went flying to her mouth. What had possessed her? It must be the tension—the air thick with passion that still hovered like an invisible encirclement about them. Eyes huge, she gazed across the table. 'I was just remembering,' she said, a hand going out entreatingly, 'an advertisement on T.V. at home, about something being cooked in spices and herbs. Kasseem, I don't want to eat. . . .'

'Well, begin one of your lessons now, because we are both going to.' The expression upon the face across the table had changed, and suddenly, unexpectedly, in one split second, he and his cousin Ahmed could have been one. The impression was gone immediately. He had begun to eat, picking up a joint of the small bird in his fingers, spearing at salad with a fork. Perforce, Alex did the same—or tried to.

It was true. What she was eating tasted like nothing she had had before—but it was also true that she couldn't make herself swallow without effort. She pushed the food round and round upon her plate, knowing that normally she liked to eat and could make a good meal—but not tonight.

Her companion was eating, his attention fixed upon his plate. But as she watched, she saw that most of that was mechanical—makebelieve too. Slowly, he spoke, as if he had been trying to find the right words.

'I had no intention of ever allowing myself to get involved—seriously involved, that is—with a woman owning a Western heritage. I had never even expected I would want to. I had been made aware of the upheaval and unhappiness that can come of mixed cultures. No . . .' he held up a restraining hand as she began to interrupt, 'hear me out, Alexandra!

'Rumours abound here in the East, and I expect that as you are interested, you might try to ferret out any gossip in which I appear. . . .'

'Ferret? What a nasty word, Kasseem. And you're wrong. I've never asked about you, or spoken your name to anyone. Anyone at all! I've listened,' Alex smiled across at him. 'as hard as I could . . . whenever I could.'

'Do you know about my parents . . . my mother?' The face opposite returned no smile.

'Yusef spoke of it to Miss Maitland.'

'Did he say she could have been . . . shall I say murdered, or just done away with.' With relief, Alex saw that now he was smiling, and it could have been maliciously, as did Miss Maitland when she was amused at something outrageous.

'Yes, something like that.' Alex left the words bare. Kasseem wasn't worried about it, so what did she care?

'You know, Alexandra, to use slang, you really are something! Don't you want to know what happened to her?'

'As far as I'm concerned, it's just not relevant.' She paused, endeavouring to find the right words. 'Look how you've behaved to me. If you were that man people whisper about, you would have taken what was so freely offered that night in Cairo when I fell head over heels in love with you, then you could have walked away. Who would have cared? Who would have blamed you? I don't care where your mother is—or what happened to her. I'll take my own chances.'

'You leave me very little defence, Alexandra . . . but actually, she is in England. Very well provided for—as long as she speaks to no one of the Omair tribe. And that, I expect, she is careful about doing. For, apart from the allowance, she is just too frightened of their reputation to risk a visit from any of them.'

'Why in heaven's name is it not known?' Anger at

the thought of him being wrongly accused made her
tone harsh.

'We, that is the tribe of the Omair, don't want it
known. Ahmed's father, the ruling Sheikh, would far
rather murder was suspected, or for that matter any
other outlandish story, than that a woman should
have been allowed to depart from home and husband. We have, as I have already told you, that reputation of ours to consider. In the region, wild desert
as well as cultivated oasis, in which we live, the
standing of the Omair is a very necessary requisite.'

Remembering the young man, Ahmed, Alex could
quite believe that he thought it was needed—and
that also it was quite probably earned.

'Take those combs out of your hair!'

Astonished at this abrupt change of subject, and
also at the tone in which the request was couched,
Alex touched her head. Possibly her hair was untidy;
they had been all through that vast temple, and had
been standing in the breeze at the bow of the
launch.

'Is it all over the place? I'll comb it,' somewhat
breathlessly she answered.

'It is not because it needs attention. I like to see it
loose.'

Colour, bright scarlet, swept up from her throat
to stain her face. She remembered when he had seen
it loose—when she had been in his arms with nothing
on but a thin toweling robe. Nevertheless, she withdrew the two pink combs and laid them upon the
table, shaking her head. Bright shining hair tumbled
about her face and shoulders.

Glancing at him, she couldn't read his expression.
His eyelids had fallen in their customary droop. Her
hand went out to him entreatingly.

His seat was pushed back, and in two strides he was around the small table, pulling her up to him. There was no hesitation, no searching, even no tenderness. This time he was kissing her with the want, the need . . . and yes, the expertise of a passion let loose, after being too tightly reined. And at last, also, she could return it, desire yielding to desire, passion to meet leaping passion, feeling the heartbeats against which she was so closely pressed begin to thunder like the hoofbeats that had sounded yesterday as his kinsmen passed by.

But unexpectedly, in a movement that brought an inarticulate protest from her, she was set aside, head resting across the arm supporting her, the shining brightness of the tumbling hair cascading all about them, her face transported, eyes hazed with emotion.

'Alexandra. . . .' His eyes, brilliance pinpointing the green, glanced directly into hers. 'Alexandra,' he repeated, 'if we continue this our boats are burned. You understand? You do understand what I'm saying?'

Unspeaking, she only nodded, and was swung up into his arms. Kasseem was descending the narrow steps into the stateroom. Across it he walked, her head resting content now upon his shoulder, allowing these golden minutes to pass over her.

The door of the bedroom kicked shut behind them, he slackened his hold so that she went down against him, and, as she had done earlier up upon the deck, she stepped on tiptoe to clasp her hands behind his neck. His lips came down to rest on each shut eyelid, before beginning their plundering march south. Bypassing her mouth, they slid along her throat, then farther to the beginning of the hollow that the cyclamen edge of the grey dress covered.

Encircling them was only silence as they remained clasped, immobile . . . one body, reality departing as the slow creeping flame turned every nerve into a raging forest fire.

A sentence came then, deep in his throat, and it was in Arabic.

Alex found herself lifted and Kasseem was moving towards the bed. On the very instant of depositing her there, abruptly, he stopped. And she knew without understanding that a new dimension had entered the room—entered also into the passion, the desire, that had engulfed them.

The launched rocked; she hadn't heard the bump against it that had penetrated senses more accustomed to outside dangers than hers. Light footsteps raced down the accommodation ladder and there came a knock upon the door, and Mustafa spoke in quick, nervous Arabic.

This time it was downwards that Alex was swung, and set away from Kasseem. Admitting Mustafa, he listened, then reached behind to pull shut the bedroom door.

'Tidy your hair, Alexandra, if you can manage it.' The tone coming from the man by her side was strange, almost unrecognisible as Kasseem's. She herself remained still, unable yet to make the descent from the fierce clamouring of desire to the mundane scene in the brightly-lit stateroom.

Other footsteps were at the top of the steps now, beginning to descend. Mustafa moved swiftly to block them, facing upwards, his back to his master. Alex put both hands up to push back the unruly hair from a face not rosy and star-flushed now, but

pale, almost frightened at these unlooked-for inter-
ruptions.

Into the space about Mustafa came the stark
white, immaculate person of Ahmed. He glanced at
the servant barring his way, and smiled. Alex
shivered, but Mustafa stood there unmoving. A
finger was raised, and a presence behind Ahmed
edged past.

'I wouldn't. . . .' The tone of the two words spoken
in English made the merest tremor of Alex's previous
shiver. It was unbelievable that it had been from
Kasseem's mouth that they had issued.

For a few moments more, silence encircled the
charged atmosphere of the room. Then, 'Move aside,
Mustafa,' said his master.

Walking down his unimpeded path, the young
Arab stopped before the owner of this place and the
girl standing beside him, then, hand to forehead, lips,
and heart, made a deep obeisance. Watching him,
Alex saw that it wasn't performed in any other way
except that of homage. 'My honoured father would
be most displeased, my cousin, that any ill-disposed,
or low-born, could enter so easily into your presence,'
the newcomer said.

'But no ill-disposed, or low-born, would dare to
try to enter my presence—or disrupt my privacy.
Enough of this play-acting, Ahmed. The reason,
please, for your appearance. In English. . . .' he
interrupted the staccato Arabic that was resounding
about them.

The eyes in this young man's face were not deep
brown, either, Alex noted. Yellow, like a hawk's, she
decided angrily, knowing also that this was unjust.
They were brimming with laughter.

Another low obeisance was proffered. 'There

has been a telephone call from Cairo. . . .'

Interrupted again before he could continue, Kasseem spoke. 'My father is there. Presumably he could deal with any phone calls.'

'But this one, my cousin, was from someone who wanted to have speech with you alone, someone to whom even my honoured uncle has to defer. It has been explained to this important man that you are out checking last-minute details for the security of his guests. You are to ring back—when we find you—for some further instructions. The line to Cairo is being kept open.'

It was in Arabic, that muttered expletive from beside her, so low that Alex could barely hear it. The young Arab undoubtedly must have. A smile touched his lips now, complementing the one dancing in those falcon's eyes.

'Yes, I absolutely agree,' he said, and Kasseem's eyelids flew wide open. A reluctant smile came also to soften the harshness of his expression.

'Very well. Tell my father that I will be there'—a hand came up and a watch was glanced at—'in under two hours.'

It was Ahmed's eyebrows that were lifted instead of his lids, and again, for that minute fraction, Alex saw Kasseem mirrored. Then the fleeting expression was gone. 'Two hours! It would surely not take me that long to find and convey you home. It was Ahmed ben Omair sent to locate you—not some servant!'

Amusement was wiped from the older man's face. 'You will return and inform them that I will be there in two hours. I am taking Miss Pembroke back to her hotel, and will then take the car home. You can go, Ahmed. . . . Mustafa?'

'It *is* important, Kasseem!' The laughter had also disappeared from the young Arab's look. 'Why else did you think I came myself?'

'I still intend to escort Miss Pembroke home. She is inclined to fall into all kinds of dilemmas. I want to have the assurance that she is where she should be before I leave Luxor. I have told you! You may go!'

'I could escort Miss Pembroke.' Hearing the words, involuntarily Alex moved closer to the re-assuring body of Kasseem. This young Arab had not even glanced her way. For the entire period of his presence on the launch, he had not only ignored her, he had acted completely as if his cousin was alone. She didn't want to have anything to do with him.

The man by her side remained silent. Then, 'Leave us . . . wait on deck,' he said.

Ahmed gave another of his low obeisances before he and his familiar went up the steps without answering. Mustafa, after a glance at his master, followed.

'I don't want to go with Ahmed. Kasseem. He frightens me,' said Alex, and saw the lopsided smile he sometimes gave to her make its appearance.

'Alexandra. . . .' the last syllable of her name went high in astonishment. 'Frightened of Ahmed? He is like my second self. I would trust anybody belonging to me to his care. Important as this business is, important as this call I have to make is, I would see you safely home myself before I made it—except that I have Ahmed to do so in my place. I would trust you with him, as I would trust my own life to him. In the desert we grew up together, and since I was eight years older than he, it was I who put him on his first horse. I taught him to shoot. He is only my second cousin, but he is closer to me than my own brother.'

Alex heard what he was saying; she knew she would recollect it later, but just now the words were washing over her. Kasseem had said, 'Anybody belonging to me'. He had said that! Never before had he actually put into words a suggestion of any kind of permanency, whatever his actions had implied. He was continuing now and she endeavoured to take in the gist of his swiftly uttered sentences.

'Ahmed is right, Alexandra—I do have to go. Look,' the words came out even faster, as if he was trying to think and plan at the same time, 'Ahmed will see you home—right home, you understand? I don't want any repetition of the Cairo incident. I want my mind freed from outside worries for the next four days.

'Mustafa will keep in touch with you, but I don't expect, knowing the pace of business here in Egypt, that Miss Maitland's affairs will be finalised before I return from the desert.

'Even if, too, we are both in Cairo at the same time, there is no way I would be able to manage even a few hours to myself. I will have people around me always until this entire project is settled. I might also have to—no, make that, I probably will, be leaving the country for a while.

'Oh, of all the confounded times for us to be flung together, why did it have to be now? Still . . .' from above her came a laugh so low as to be almost only the sliver of a chuckle, 'although I have never thought of myself as a devious man, I have prepared some surprises that I hope will solve all my problems.'

Alex was listening and she was hearing, but also

she was trying to impress an imprint on her memory. With all the important people Kasseem would be surrounded by, these next few days. With all the manipulation and dealing that presumably he would be involved in, could her small image be cancelled out.

Her shoulders were caught and she was shaken, not gently, either. In astonishment, her expression changed. 'That's better,' said Kasseem's voice. 'You looked as if you were going to a funeral, and allow me to assure you that neither mine nor your own is contemplated. With Machiavellian thoroughness I have been sowing seeds, and if they grow as well as I think they will, there should be some happy endings. But your place in my life is fixed—whatever eventuates. Do you hear me?'

Switching to Arabic, his voice was hardly audible.

'What does that mean?' she asked.

'I couldn't say it to you in English, the way things stand. And anyway, it sounds much better in flowery Arabic that it ever could in cold English.

'Now, give me one of those brilliant smiles that was the thing that caught at my attention in that damned airport. On what slender threads do our destinies rest!'

His tone had dropped and she was pulled close against him, and as his head came down, on tiptoe she stretched to meet it. For a few seconds, a few minutes, so they remained, Alex with her mouth against his lips, savouring love, desire, passion. Kasseem not allowing the moment to go beyond control. As she was set back, he said, as if trying to force common sense before the passion that held them both in thrall, 'Don't doubt me, Alexandra. I've handled more complex problems in my time. Come, up on deck.'

Perforce, she followed him up into the cockpit and almost out on to the open deck he swung round suddenly, returning to where the table had been set. 'Here,' he told her, holding out the two pink combs, 'tidy your hair. I'm quite happy to see it in that condition; I don't expect others to do the same.'

'Oh, Kasseem, what an Arabic way of thinking! A little disorder—who would know, who would care?'

'I would know, I would care. And of course I have an Arab way of thinking. Whatever you may have been told, whatever impressions you may have gained from our association, I *am* an Arab. Think of that in the time we're separated.'

'Yes, my lord Kasseem, I'll do just that,' said Alex, performing a deep curtsey before him. 'There won't be a minute when I'm not thinking of you.'

They were outside before he could answer her, joining Ahmed and his servant. Arabic echoed back and forth, then without even a glance in her direction, her beloved had climbed nimbly down into a small boat which chugged quickly away.

Alex watched it as long as it was visible. She turned then to the young man whom, despite Kasseem's blessing, she was still very wary of. The launch's engine had started, Mustafa was at the wheel and with a wide turn, they were heading back to Luxor.

'It might be more comfortable if we go under the awning to sit down, Miss Pembroke.' Ahmed's English was not as accent-free as his cousin's. But in other circumstances Alex knew that she might have found it attractive. However, not now, and not from this young Arab. He had called her Miss Pembroke. Had it been from reports or had it been from Kasseem's calling her that tonight?

As they sat at the table, all the uneaten food caught at her gaze. Unexpectedly, Ahmed's glance rose suddenly from the same source to meet her look, and she felt her face flaming. Implicit in his eyes had been understanding of the reason for the neglected meal. Her back straightened, her gaze drifted to the coolness of indifference. What right had this boy to own such knowledge? He would be lucky if he was actually out of his teens, most likely not as old as her own twenty years. And whatever experiences he had indulged in, falling in love with Kasseem had been the first and only time she had been caught up in this maelstrom of emotion.

As she looked at him, at the fierce eyes that reminded her of a falcon's, the lids came down. Just like Kasseem! thought Alex, incensed. Then he spoke, and both words and tone were devoid of anything but the making of polite conversation.

'Were you impressed by the temple, Miss Pembroke, by the soaring bulk of it? I never ride past without wondering at the motive for its construction. I myself prefer our outer oases where we live in tents. The palace headquarters where my father rules I visit as little as I am allowed. Buildings stifle me.'

'Yes, I can imagine that the wilder it is, the better you would like it,' Alex retorted a trifle acidly.

The young man laughed, and unexpectedly she found she could like him, however warily she might tread in his vicinity.

'What shall I call you?' she asked. She had wondered that about Kasseem too, she remembered. 'Is it Sheikh Ahmed?'

'If it wouldn't offend you, you could merely call me Ahmed.'

'Would that be . . .?' Alex hesitated. She didn't really know how to handle this young man. Then came so clearly the memory of Kasseem's voice saying, 'He is like my other self.' So, 'Would it be in order for me to do that? I don't know what's done and not done here, as I would automatically know at home.'

'Yes, I think it would be quite in order for you to call me Ahmed. My cousin would approve. Is that what you were wondering?' Ahmed wasn't smiling at her now. Even those eyes of his showed gravity.

Alex nodded. 'Would it also be in order,' she continued, 'for you to call me Alex? Would you cousin approve of that?'

Ahmed did smile then, a boy's genuine grin, his bow going quite low was as graceful as if he had been standing before her, instead of being seated at the littered table. This bow was not in any way an obeisance; that mark of respect, thought Alex, would be kept for the elderly, and important men.

'Alex?' he said, and the word carried a different inflection from any other way she had heard her name spoken. 'Kasseem does not call you that.'

It was Alex's turn to smile. 'No. Miss Maitland with whom I came to Egypt has always called me Alexandra. Everyone else I know calls me Alex. I expect that as Miss Maitland introduced me as Alexandra, that is what Kasseem calls me.'

'Then I had better only call you Alex, hadn't I, if the other is Kasseem's own name for you?'

This time her answering smile was friendly, reserve and wariness hidden away. Still, she wondered at his ease with her, and the modern way he caught on to nuances, thinking that he must have known other European girls. He hadn't learnt his expert give and take in the secluded and chaperoned area where Arab girls of his class existed. Casually, she enquired, 'Do you come up to Luxor or Cairo often, or do you spend all your life in the desert?'

'I come to both cities a few times a year; mostly on business. I also, like your own countrymen do on holiday, come to enjoy the pleasures of the city and relax. I have my own . . . company,' had he hesitated before describing what it was he had?—'for the Omair trade a lot—south to the Sudan, east to . . .' he stopped suddenly, then ended prosaically, 'Oh, all over the place. We breed horses that are famous and known all over the world, did you know that?'

She had not known it. However, after taking note of the beautiful mounts that he and his followers had ridden, Alex could well believe that piece of information.

'We deal in other commodities besides the mundane ones of camels and horses, hides and dates. Maybe one day Kasseem will give you a memento of some of our more exotic trading.' Amusement was back again behind those hooded eyes.

'Yes . . . well. . . .' was all she could find to answer on that subject. She didn't want to know any of the Omair trading secrets, if that was what the less than open explanation that Ahmed had provided meant. Then, unexpectedly, astonished that the time had passed so quickly, she saw they were edging into the jetty at Luxor.

They were met, and Arabic between the two Arabs on board, and the two who stepped forward to meet the launch, echoed back and forth. The language sounded angry, violent even. Alex stood off to one side, resolutely disengaging herself from this conflict, and beside her stood Mustafa, silent also.

The whole scene was abruptly finished. From Ahmed there came a tone that left nothing to the imagination. He was the ruler now; the Sheikh Ahmed ben Omair, son of the paramount chief, giving orders, his boy's face chilled, stone-hard. Into the ensuing silence Ahmed turned to her. 'Please to go,' he addressed her. 'I will see you home.'

Again Alex trod down what was becoming very familiar territory, and up on to the bank of the Nile. Back to the hotel she went, with Ahmed and his young men on either side: the two bearded tribesmen of the Omair a few paces behind.

Whatever would they say at the hotel when the entire lot of them crowded into the entrance? Alex worried, searching round in her mind for a reason to dispose of the whole lot of them.

Passing the new Winter Palace, still a blaze of light, echoing with laughter and the sound of tourists enjoying themselves, they came to what Miss Maitland called the icing-sugar cake. 'Thank you, Ahmed,' Alex said then, turning to dismiss him. 'Maybe one day in the future we'll meet again.' She didn't put out her hand. She merely smiled.

But an arm swung from out the voluminous robes towards the steps of the pink façade. 'I will see you inside,' said Ahmed curtly, so the five of them walked sedately up the few short steps. Again at the entrance, Alex turned, irritability and distress fighting for supremacy. Ahmed gave only the barest of movements and a white-robed figure moved round to hold open the door wider.

Praying the lounge might be empty, without any expectation that it would be so early in the night, of necessity, she went ahead. At least only the two younger Arabs followed: the other two remaining at the entrance, absolutely indifferent to the curious glances they were receiving.

Wishing to get the whole episode over as quickly as possible. Alex marched straight through and up the steps leading to the corridor in which her room was situated. There was no key to be collected. Kasseem had only pulled shut her door.

They reached it, and this time she turned definitely to say goodbye. A finger was raised again, and the young man who had remained unspoken all night as far as Alex could remember reached round and opened the door.

'Doesn't he do anything for himself?' muttered Alex under her breath, and then remembered how he had handled his horse yesterday.

'Safe in your room, my cousin ordered. Goodnight!' Ahmed raised a hand, and turning without more ado had departed.

## CHAPTER EIGHT

AWAYS afterwards, Alex remembered the next four days as dream-hazed. She went places; she did things, but it was as if some other person did them. Her inside self took no part.

It was with a jump that she came out of bed the next morning, almost with alarm. Then the sound that had woken her penetrated deeper. Helicopters, four or five of them, were passing directly over the hotel, the noise vibrating all around. She took a step to the small window, craning her head every way, and was in time to see the awkward, unwieldy flying birds disappear. One of them carried Kasseem, she knew. She glanced at her small travelling clock. Help! Past nine o'clock. What was Miss Maitland thinking?

Grabbing hold of a cotton dressing gown, Alex opened her door and walked the few paces to her companion's room. Giving a quick tap, she turned the handle and finding it unlocked, went inside.

'I'm sorry, Miss Maitland,' she began, 'I over-slept.'

'I know, Alexandra. I had someone go and look, but I told them not to disturb you. I'm not dressed, either, as you can see. I'm having my breakfast here, have you had anything to eat?'

'No, I haven't.' The question was waved away, and sitting on the edge of the bed, Alex smiled across at the wrinkled face. 'Tell me,' she asked, 'how did things go yesterday?'

'First, ring for some breakfast. I can talk while we both eat.'

Reluctantly, nevertheless, Alex picked up Miss Maitland's phone—she didn't have one in her own small room—and ordered tea, toast, and orange juice, then settled back and enquired again. 'How *did* things go?'

'Surprisingly well,' was the answer. 'You'll love the little boy. He has such a look of Norma about him, even though he is of the opposite sex. And he's not very dark, either. The little girl is—dark, I mean. More like her father. However, she's a pretty little thing, and already speaks good English. Raschid says Norma always spoke in English with her. . . .' As if remembering, Miss Maitland was silent for a moment, then sighed, before continuing.

'We've hammered out some sort of an agreement.

Old Robber Baron Yusef is down here and tomorrow I'm going to look over a tract of land. If I think it suitable, and if my lawyers do too—well, we'll see. I'm taking my time, because I've decided to see if I can possibly persuade Raschid to come back to Australia with me. But I have to progress very carefully.'

'Raschid to come home with you . . . to Australia?' Astonishment caused Alex's voice to rise. 'He'd never do that! His whole family is here . . . his life. . . .'

'I'm not mentioning it yet, but everything I do and say is angled towards that end. I like him, Alexandra. He has two older brothers and two sisters, he wouldn't be sorely missed, so . . .' Miss Maitland grinned that malicious grin of hers to Alex, 'I'm working on it.'

'Devious, that's what you are,' Alex scolded, and even as she did so, knew the word was familiar. Kasseem had used it last night in regard to himself. However, she thought decidedly, whatever else Kasseem was, deviousness had no part in his make-up, but it had in this old woman's. Alex shook her head across at her, then rose to open the door as her breakfast arrived.

Comfortably they sat eating together, Alex with her tray upon her lap, Miss Maitland at her small table. Alex had no intention of mentioning Kasseem, or last night at all, if she could help it. She knew with certainty that no one, no staff, that was, would be gossiping concerning it, and in the unlikely event of one of the guests mentioning it to Miss Maitland, she intended to shrug it off as the guide obtained for her. Heavens! Kasseem a guide. Inside herself she laughed.

'After lunch, Raschid is calling for us. You'll

probably enjoy walking over cotton fields and among date palms—and seeing a real Egyptian home.'

'Yes, Miss Maitland. Do you want me? I mean, need me? Of course I'll come if that's the case. That, after all, is why I'm here. But actually, I have a headache, and if you don't mind I'd prefer to stay home. Perhaps tomorrow. . . .' Alex glanced rather anxiously across the room. She knew her companion well enough to realise she would know at once if she was wanted.

She encountered an equally anxious look. 'Is it only a headache, Alexandra? You have to be careful in places like these. I wouldn't want you to get sick. I don't know how I would have managed without you through the entire trip. You made it so much easier for me.' Praise indeed from a woman who indulged in only practical utterances.

Relaxed, Alex walked the few yards and bent to lay her hand upon the upright shoulder. 'I'm perfectly well, though a little tired. Also, my hair needs washing, and I have laundry to do. And you have Raschid to escort you.'

It was almost eleven o'clock when she returned to her own room. She dressed, washed some clothes, even the grey dress, leaving it to drip-dry over the bathtub. It had brushed against, and been brushed by, stones and columns and people last night, and she wanted it fresh to hang away.

Raschid came to collect his aunt by marriage, and back in her room, Alex wondered at the feeling of lethargy that she couldn't seem to shake off. She pushed a chair into the sunshine spilling through her window and sat there to dry her just washed hair. Once home—if she went home—she would buy the brand of shampoo Kasseem had so casually thrown into the bathtub on the launch. It would be another aid to a memory that wouldn't need it.

She combed her hair and rolled it in rollers, not bothering to get up and go about all the things that needed doing. She just sat. She ate dinner by herself, then went to bed, expecting not to sleep at all . . . and drifted off immediately. She didn't know, as doctors do, that nature has its own way of repairing the abuse that tension and stretched nerves could cause.

It was early when she awoke next morning and she went directly to Miss Maitland's room.

'Oh, good, Alexandra—I'm glad you're here,' was her greeting. 'You look healthy enough too, thank goodness. Now, I've got a lot to do today, Mr Yusef is coming to talk business, which suits me very well now. Whether it will suit him is another matter. I'll be away the entire day, but will be home to have dinner with you.

'And if things go through as I expect them to do, we could be off tomorrow, or definitely the day after. So why don't you go on a tour to this Valley of the Kings they talk about? You wouldn't want to miss those old tombs, especially the classic of them all, Tutankhamen's tomb, while you're actually here, now would you? So be off to get dressed and we'll have breakfast.'

Returning from the new Winter Palace dining room after their meal, Alex left her companion and walked across to the desk in their own part of the hotel. Smiling at the clerk behind it. She enquired about the tour to the Valley of the Kings.

'Certainly we have one going today, Miss Pembroke,' she was told. 'It leaves at ten o'clock. Shall I book you on it?'

'Yes, please. Do I wait here in the lounge?'

'Yes, tourists for the tours are collected here. And oh, Miss Pembroke, there is a guide free who would be glad to be of service. It's hard trekking in the valley, and the hotel would feel better if you had someone of your own. . . .'

'I shouldn't expect that will be necessary. . . .' Alex was beginning, smiling, then she stopped. The atmosphere seemed funny, strange.

'There will be no extra charge; it is just a hotel service—to carry your bag and see that you don't miss anything.'

A thought intruded into Alex's mind, and she looked directly at the dark face opposite. It gazed just as blankly back at her.

Shrugging, she turned away, calling over her shoulder, 'Very well,' thinking that maybe it was just the hotel looking after a top paying guest like Miss Maitland. If it was something to do with Kasseem . . . well, what did it matter? She decided she was being silly, though, surmising it had to do with him. Thousands of tourists made this tour every year and probably quite a few of them had independent guides.

For the second morning she waved her companion and Raschid away, then turned to find the reception clerk at her elbow. 'This is Mohammed, Miss Pembroke. He will make your trip to the Valley of the Kings more pleasant.'

He doesn't belong to the Omair tribe, anyway, I was just imagining things earlier, thought Alex to herself, as she greeted him. Mohammed was a tall grave Egyptian, dressed in the usual ankle-length gown, clean-shaven, and speaking only when necessary.

Once upon a time, Alex knew, to visit this famous

place would be the highlight of any journey. Today, she only went through the motions, finding neither energy or enthusiasm.

Across the river to the west bank they chugged, then were taken along a road through the pass into what is called the Valley of the Kings. This was not a terrain that would call forth visions of a valley for most people; a place of green fields separated by glistening water flowing placidly. Harshness met the gaze here, of rocks burning yellow, scorching to the touch, their shadows blue cobalt. Only the brilliant azure of the sky, a colour so deep, so pure, it would always remain an incredible memory of Egypt, brought relief.

They walked and saw, and listened—and wondered. . . . How could anyone expect to have their belongings, their jewels, their wealth, transported to where they were going after death? These men had not been primitive people. How could this cult of ensuring their high place in the hereafter have started? Alex shrugged—and then of course they stood beside the most famous tomb of all.

'Yes, this is the burial place of the young Pharaoh Tutankhamen. And yes,' their guide was continuing, 'he does still sleep here!' He was rewarded for these words by an uneasy rustling among his charges. Alex glanced at her own 'guide' who had remained two paces behind her throughout the tour. His face was blandly grave, a man merely listening.

'Archaeologists,' their guide was continuing, 'excited beyond measure at unearthing a tomb practically unlooted, took years to sift and transfer the furnishing and treasures to the Cairo museum, but they replaced the young king in his coffin, and here he sleeps still, in that sarcophagus there.'

Dismissing the peculiarities which men practised over three thousand years ago, they trailed back to the new rest-house for lunch, and to Alex, the day, the sights, began to coalesce until the temple of Deir el Bahri almost brought back her interest. She thought it beautiful, but was glad when they were finally on the river again, homeward bound. At least it was cool here.

Thinking of a bath, a cold drink, as they neared the hotel she almost didn't see the car swish close to draw up before the pink steps.

'Alex, just a moment!' a voice called, and she swung round. Raschid had alighted from the car and was depositing a little girl on to the pavement, before turning back to help Miss Maitland.

Alex and the small girl looked at one another. 'Hello, are you Yasmin?' asked Alex.

'Yes,' reluctantly, shyly, the answer came.

Alex bent down and swung her up, hugging her close. 'I'm your Aunty Alex, Yasmin. Can you say Aunty Alex?'

Standing the little one back on her feet, she knelt down, smiling into the small face. Yasmin was more like her father than Norma, as her great-aunt had already said. Although she wasn't as dark as Raschid, she had his black curly hair and large brown eyes. Those eyes gazed at the grey ones looking at her, and suddenly they smiled, lit up, and a quiet voice said, 'Aunty Alex.'

It could have been an Australian voice speaking; no accent at all was discernible. Alex glanced swiftly up to where Raschid was standing with the older woman, to meet his smile.

'Norma spoke English to her from the moment she was born, and I've continued it. That was what her mother wished—she also speaks Arabic, though, of course.'

Alex rose from her kneeling position, still holding on to one of the small hands. 'She's lovely, isn't she, Miss Maitland? Aren't you lucky?'

A complacent nod was all she received in answer.

'Well now, Raschid has to get home. He's going to be a busy person, and I want to hear all about your day. . . .' Miss Maitland paused, interrupted, as the silent Egyptian beside Alex moved to hand over the large carryall.

She wasn't the only one whose attention was upon him. Sideways, Alex caught the look that he was receiving from Raschid. An intent expression coloured the young Egyptian's countenance as he glanced from Mohammed to Alex, then back again. More thoughtfully he looked at the hand extending the bag, and almost shook his head as his gaze swung again to the tall grave figure in the long robe.

The tiny incident was past, and Raschid remained silent. Mohammed bowed, and before Alex could begin to tip him, he had walked away.

'Was that your guide, or what Raschid calls your dragoman?' asked Miss Maitland. 'He certainly seems much quieter than the majority we've had foisted upon us. Now, come along. Goodbye, Raschid, until tomorrow.' She patted the little girl's head, and took hold of Alex's arm.

They mounted the steps, and as she turned to wave as the car drew away, almost a gasp escaped Alex's lips. The sun was setting on the western side of the river right opposite, splashing the cliffs and rocks on that side with brightness and shadow. But there was no shadow on the river. From the low bank of crimson fire that was the horizon came the

colour which flooded the waters on the Nile with
gold and scarlet. It was incredible—the vividness,
the intensity. A sunset anywhere from now on,
ordinary or not, would always bring her back to the
steps of the old Winter Palace.

It was a movement from the woman by her side
that broke the spell. 'I know your propensity for
romantic sights and places, Alexandra, and, even if
I also recognise this as something worth looking at, I
want to get to my room. It's been a long hard day of
negotiating.

'Now,' she said, subsiding into a chair, 'we're
going to have the best dinner with the best champagne that this hotel can provide. But first, Raschid
is coming home with us. . . .' she held up a hand to
silence the incipient interruption.

'I've bought a large tract of land—at least, old
Yusef——' Alex hid a grin. 'Old Yusef' was
probably twenty years younger than this woman
sitting so complacently across from her, who, dislik-
ing the lawyer from that first interview, always spoke
of him in derogatory terms, '—bought it for me. I'm
sending the papers home to my lawyers for verifica-
tion. I've signed the cheque for the deposit, however.
It's to be in Raschid's and my nephew's name, but
joins the family complex. We've agreed that if
Raschid doesn't find himself content with Australia,
he's free to come home.

'You know, Alexandra,' here Miss Maitland
paused for a moment, 'the family here is a very important entity, much more so than at home. But
we've worked it out. I'm happy, Raschid's family is
happy, as I hope Raschid will be in Australia. It
won't be my fault if he isn't. I like him.'

'It's turned out better than you expected, hasn't

it? I'm so glad. I think Yasmin is a charming little girl,' Alex grinned at the face opposite, but her tone was chiding. 'You only like her, don't you? It's the baby boy you love. That's wrong!'

'You can't help whom you love, you should know that. . . .' Alex had swung her head round abruptly, searching for a double meaning to those only too true words. But the sentence had been innocent as far as she was concerned. Miss Maitland had no knowledge of Kasseem.

'However,' the older woman was continuing slowly, 'although you can't help where your feelings take you, you should try to show no favouritism. I will try!

'Now, enough of this. Off to your room to bathe and dress. Hand me that phone before you go, and I'll ring through to order dinner. Now that everything is over bar the signing, I feel as if a weight had lifted, so be off with you—and dress up a bit.'

Alex handed over the phone, and in her own room, stood under the cascading water of the shower, wondering where Kasseem was, what he was doing, and if he was thinking of her. Was he preparing for dinner as she was and saying what a waste of time to be drinking champagne with someone else? She didn't even want to get dressed up, but for Miss Maitland's sake she was going to.

It wasn't only a long dinner, either, it was going to end up a long night too, she thought resignedly when her companion accepted an invitation to join a group of Americans whose laughter and enjoyment were already resounding throughout the lounge.

What a thing was attraction, thought Alex. If she hadn't met Kasseem she would have thoroughly enjoyed herself tonight, because as many men as women were in this group of Americans, and more than one of the masculine gender gravitated to her side. She smiled and talked, and with a competence she had always possessed, dealt with the passes flung her way. Her other self sat outside all of it and though of another man, whose merest touch brought the dull world around her alive with pulsing colour.

'Did you know, Alex, that you can hire horses to ride out into the desert in the early mornings?' asked a man whose name she had not gathered in the casually uttered introductions. 'Shall I order two for us? It will add the finishing touch to our trip before we have to leave. Just think of it—the two of us alone out there in the romantic desert,' he was half whispering into her ear.

'Yes, I can just imagine it,' she replied, laughing, and eased herself away, placing distance between his leaning over figure and her own body. She caught her companion's glance and raised an eyebrow. Receiving a nod, thankfully she rose, saying, 'We're off to bed, I'm afraid, but it's been lovely to have met you all. Enjoy the rest of your trip, especially those of you who go riding into the desert.' Warmly, she sent her smile to flash around the entire group, then took hold of Miss Maitland's arm.

'Did you want to stay on?' she enquired, as they walked slowly along to their rooms. 'I think that tour today made me tired—also, I was very bored.'

'No, Alexandra, I did want to have a celebration dinner. But suddenly I'm tired too. I hope Raschid gets the tickets for tomorrow's plane. All I want to do now is get home.'

To herself, Alex said, I'll think about that later when I'm alone. And later, dropping on to her bed, she did think about it. Mustafa hadn't contacted her

... but what if Mohammed belonged to Kasseem? Anyway, whatever they did, Kasseem would know. Hadn't he said the Omair knew everything that went on in Egypt? She would go to bed and see what tomorrow brought.

And tomorrow came as it always did. Searching through a small window, a ray of light found the eyelids of a figure sleeping in a tossed and tumbled bed. They lifted, the gaze behind them roving the room, then awareness came, and a glance at the outside world showed the cerulean Egyptian sky— not the usual brazen deep blue, but pearl-hazed, giving to it a luminosity unseen except in the early morning. The rays of a just risen sun would soon come into their own to scorch the whole land and bring to life the vividness of its colours, the intensity of blazing brightness, ebony shade, lapis lazuli skies, the emerald of green, the burning gold of the desert sands—the world where Kasseem was.

Alex turned away from the window and pulled a pillow over her head, recalling his face as it had come down to kiss her. She shook her head; she wouldn't think of that. However, she brought to memory the few times she had been with him, of his immaculate, aloof white presence at the airport; in the passion-filled room on the launch as he had walked out and left her. And most of all, on the rooftop of Shepheards Hotel when he had silently laughed at her, and called himself the wicked Sheikh. That ... that was the first time this unlikely love affair had come to have solidity and background.

She remembered the temple where he had also laughed at her for thinking that Nefertiti's statue could possibly have been standing in that particular building, and had said that he had no interest in building monuments to any religious ideals, but in building a better life for ordinary people.

Every word he had uttered she would remember . . . and himself. The way his lids fell suddenly half-closed to hide thoughts he didn't want disclosed. His mouth, that could have been the model used for paintings over three thousand years old—clear-cut, austere. But it held, too, a hint of gentleness. . . . Suddenly another face, another mouth, imposed itself upon the one she was thinking of. This mouth also could have been inherited from ancestors aeons away in time. It too, was clear-cut, but it was not austere, and it certainly held no hint of gentleness. It did hold ruthlessness—Ahmed's!

Wasn't she lucky she had fallen in love with Kasseem, even if nothing ever came of it? Ahmed was the other side of love's coin.

Alex twisted restlessly. Would they be leaving Luxor today? Tomorrow Kasseem came in from the desert and was going straight to Cairo. He had told her he would be too involved with important nego-tiations to see her, but surely he would send a mes-sage with Mustafa. . . .

Again she twisted restlessly, then drew a deep breath and swung her legs sideways. Nothing could come of lying here thinking; that was the way tension built up. She would shower and dress and go to Miss Maitland . . . and later wander round the places in Luxor that she knew and say goodbye.

# CHAPTER NINE

IT was as they had just entered Miss Maitland's room after breakfast that the knock came on the door. Alex had been upset, and angry too, when she had gone to collect her companion for the morning meal.

Good heavens, Miss Maitland, you look awful . . . in fact you look ill. You're not to get up. I think you should stay in bed.'

She had received a shake of the head. 'I'm not ill, Alexandra. Not as I was in Athens. In fact, as I've remarked before, I've been singularly free of pain in Egypt. Still, I'm tired, and depending on whether we're leaving for Cairo today or not, I'll rest.' Alex eased her into a chair now, then went to answer the door.

'It's a letter from Raschid. Shall I open it?' Receiving a nod, she slit the envelope.

'Dear Aunt Elizabeth,' she read. 'I am unable to book us on today's plane. We leave at ten-thirty tomorrow. As I have a great deal to do, I will not see you today, but will collect you and Alex at nine-thirty in the morning. Until then, dear Aunt Elizabeth,

Your nephew,
Raschid.

He sounds as if he was pleased and happy about coming events,' Alex commented.

'Yes, I do really think he is.'

Ruthlessly, Alex stripped down the bed quilt and placed a hand under the frail elbow. 'Now we know we're not leaving, rest time for you. Come along!'

'You look so fierce, Alexandra. I'd be frightened to obstruct you.'

Alex laughed. 'I know how frightened you are of anyone! But we have nothing special to do today, so a morning's rest won't hurt you.' She reached down to strip off the old lady's shoes, then plumped pillows behind the upright shoulders. 'Have you had your pills?' she asked.

'I don't want any pills. I'll just sit up here and enjoy watching you stamp around in the room like an elephant on the rampage.'

Alex laughed. She had just tipped out one of the large suitcases, preparatory to repacking it. Turning to ask a question when she had almost finished, she moved quietly across, taking away one of the high pillows and easing the sleeping figure down flat.

She ate lunch by herself. Finishing her lamb chop and salad, she ordered an omelette and fresh fruit salad to be sent to Miss Maitland's room, then wended her way there.

'Oh, so you're awake. Lunch is on the way,' she told the figure already up and dressed. 'What's on the agenda for the rest of our time here?'

'We're going shopping, at those shops we looked at before.'

Whether it had been the few hours' rest, or having her affairs settled, Alex didn't know. But the afternoon passed in a whirl of shopping and laughter. She was moved to protest once, her shoulders shaking, at her companion's outrageous comments on the Egyptian salesman trying to sell her an enormous ivory elephant.

'Really, Miss Maitland, you've bought enough. It won't be you trying to pack all this, you know—it will be me! Come on, pay for all this stuff and we'll get home. . . .' She stopped suddenly, both speaking and laughing. She had called this place home. They were leaving soon. Would she ever come to call Egypt home? Would she see Kasseem . . .? He would be back in Cairo tomorrow, and so would she.

She shook her head to clear these thoughts away as Miss Maitland spoke. 'Give me my travellers' cheques, Alexandra. I might even buy this elephant if you don't keep quiet.' And that was the mood in which she remained until they finally got back to their rooms for the night.

They had had dinner with the Americans again, champagne flowing until Alex had finally said she had had enough.

'Tch, tch, Alexandra—shame on you! And we oldies still willing to make a night of it, while you want to go to bed! Oh, well, I guess it's not such a bad idea at that.'

Alex had checked, as she always did, that the older woman had all she needed before retiring, then moved the few yards down the hallway to her own room. Standing by the window, she gazed at the night; at the date palms rising high above the low-lying garden, at the dark sky pinpointed with jewelled diamonds. Then she turned away, and began on her own packing.

Walking across from breakfast for the last time, Alex settled Miss Maitland at a table writing travellers' cheques, then went to ascertain that their luggage had been collected; it had. At the mirror in her room, she took the combs from her hair, dark blue ones to match the severe blue skirt she was wearing for the journey, and ran a proper comb through to tidy it. Suddenly she bent closer, to gaze at her reflection. She hadn't noticed it before; she hadn't been looking much in mirrors lately.

Her complexion had never been lily-white; few women's in Australia ever were. However, she had never been among the bronzed brown set, either. Looking back at her was an apricot skin. Always outside in the blazing sunshine, she had worn a hat, but apart from that she had never bothered. The Egyptian sun had done its work silently. Alex smiled back at her reflection. The glowing apricot did something for her, she acknowledged, as did also, now she looked at it, the lighter blonde shade that rippled golden through her hair as she moved.

Would Kasseem notice . . . would he ever see it? She had awoken, wondering at the feeling of depression that had only deepened, not departed as the morning wore on——could it be a portent of things to come?

She shrugged, telling herself not to be stupid, and recalled the words she had hugged to herself for four days. 'Your place in my life is fixed, Alexandra. Never doubt me.'

The side-combs went in, she slung her bag across her shoulder and went through the door.

The upright figure was sitting idle now, gazing absently into the distance. Dropping down beside her, Alex asked, 'Surely not a headache from the champagne?'

'Good heavens, Alexandra—from that little lot? I've drunk wine all my life. There's a cellar at home, even yet containing stuff my father put down. Still, we turned one on last night, didn't we?'

'You might have done so. I have a perfectly clear

head. Oh——' she smiled at the woman who had
just pulled out a chair, one of their companions of
last night. Alex loved her accent. It reminded her of
that other Southern lady who had waved to her from
the horse-carriage when Kasseem was escorting her
to Karnak. Kasseem! Oh dear—would everything,
everywhere, remind her of him? She stood up
abruptly, and smiled at the two women.

'I'll go and look for Raschid, it's nine-thirty. He
should be here now.' Outside, she gazed out and
over the river. 'Goodbye, Luxor,' she said.

Brakes applied suddenly broke into her dreaming,
bringing reality sharply back. Raschid ran up the
steps. He gestured to the luggage and looked round
for a porter, but there was no need. The luggage
was already in the process of being loaded.

'This is my brother, Ramadam,' Raschid was
saying, indicating the man who had slipped out from
behind the wheel. 'We've already taken the baby
and Yasmin to the airport. Is my aunt ready?'

She was already at the top of the steps, and settled
carefully in her seat by Raschid, they were soon
driving again the road that was a wedge through the
prolific green fields on both sides.

Thankfully Alex sat on one of the forms, taking
charge of Yasmin from the nurse. Raschid could
handle things more competently here than she could.
She glanced from the baby in its cane-basket carrier
to the dark-skinned woman whose hand rested pro-
tectingly upon it. Smiling, Alex spoke to her.

The brown face shook from side to side. 'She
doesn't speak English,' said a little voice, and there
came a spate of quick Arabic from Yasmin. The
nurse nodded. 'She is only coming to Cairo with us,
Aunty Alex,' said Yasmin.

'Shall I be taking charge of the baby from there?' Alex asked Miss Maitland, and added, 'Oh, I hope I can look after him all right. I don't know very much about young babies.'

'No. Old Yusef is getting us a trained nurse from the hospital in Cairo. She's to come to Australia and stay until my nephew is acclimatized, then we'll fly her back. At least in this, he's made himself useful. . . .'

The end of her sentence was almost drowned out as their transport arrived, taxiing down the runway to pull up opposite the exit. Raschid was joining them, pushing papers into an inside jacket pocket. They began to converge on the entrance, Alex holding Yasmin's small hand tightly, when a much louder vibration made itself heard. A step more, and a face raised to the lapis lazuli infinity above showed her the helicopters flying over the far side of the airport.

So Kasseem was back. He had said four days. If only one could beam thoughts through the airwaves! Alex glanced down as Yasmin's hand tightened in hers.

'It's only helicopters, love,' she told the little girl, and turning to answer a question from Raschid, she saw Mohammed. He was standing apart from the throng of tourists and workers. She looked directly at him, but his gaze was beyond her, as if waiting.

'Silly!' she took herself to task. He had every right to be out here. There were tourists arriving on that plane; they were even passing her now. And tourists were most likely his livelihood.

They straggled across the baked earth and up the steps, Raschid helping Miss Maitland now. Alex picked up Yasmin, and with her shoulder bag bumping beside her, moved into their places.

Cairo, when they arrived, was familiar territory. There again, as well at the large motley crowd, were Arabs in their immaculate white gowns. There was no Kasseem, of course. Shepheards, also, was an old acquaintance. They waited on the wide marble floor for Raschid to register, each piece of luggage with a porter beside it. They even received some nods of recognition.

Their rooms were not on the river side this time, however, but looking out over the city. 'Come along, Yasmin,' said Alex. 'We'll just check on how your Aunt Elizabeth is settling in.' Passing the four rooms they had been allocated, Alex thought it was just as well that Miss Maitland was wealthy, for they would be here until their passports were processed. Raschid would already have his, but the children wouldn't— and probably not the new nurse, either.

'Thank goodness, Alexandra, the next departure will be the one on our way home,' they were greeted with, accompanied by a sigh of thankfulness.

'The trip up from Luxor doesn't seemed to have worried you. You look blooming,' Alex told her. 'Shall we put it down to all the late nights and all the champagne that we guzzled?'

'What an expression to use! It's simply not in my vocabulary, and I would never suppose it to be in yours,' but Miss Maitland was laughing as she added, 'You'd better not be nasty now, Alexandra. Just wait and see what I'm doing for you! Raschid has gone to get our business over with Old Yusef first. He's then going to hire an air-conditioned car complete with driver, so we can then explore this whole city and countryside while we're waiting.

'And I'll have you know that it's you principally that I'm doing it for,' she added. 'I feel guilty that you've been so good, and have been left alone so much, and have seen hardly anything of the foreign places we've been to. So if we *have* got to be here, we'll see the sights— the Pyramids, the museum, the bazaars. . . .'

Trying to hide her discomfiture at the knowledge that she had seen all she had needed, Alex broke in on all the things they were going to do, saying with a laugh, 'I'm not going with you to any bazaars, Miss Maitland. You can't fit another object in your cases! And heavens, after all you bought in Luxor, you simply can't want anything else.'

'Who said anything about want? I don't *want* anything else. But look at the fun you have buying stuff you don't want. So we'll go out and buy up the town.'

'I don't know what's come over you, Miss Maitland! You've changed beyond recognition these last few days. You'll have to stop acting as if you've been sniffing glue or getting high on LSD.'

That did bring a chuckle. Then the laughter went. 'Actually, I don't know how one feels using the two substances you mentioned, but I could be acting as if I've had more than my share of champagne. I simply didn't expect to buy what I have. I thought maybe one of the children—even if I'd come prepared to bargain away money for both. Now I've got them, and Raschid too. When Norma didn't return from England, she took part of my life with her. Now I've got some of it back again.'

'Oh, Miss Maitland!' Tears stung behind Alex's eyelids. 'Look,' she said, 'we'll make that driver earn his keep. We'll go everywhere and see everything.

Now,' to more practical subjects, 'just a little catnap until Raschid returns, eh?'

And they did go all over the place; in air-conditioned comfort too. More than they should have for Miss Maitland's health, in Alex's estimation. And—she clasped the knowledge close—there came a note from Kasseem, bought by Mustafa just before dinner on the second night. It started with Arabic script across the top, then continued abruptly in English.

'We arrived last night. I am busy. It's the palace for us this evening. Tomorrow night we—my family—are entertaining. I will try, however, to see you some time Thursday, or Thursday night. Until then, Alexandra, my love as always.

Kasseem.'

At least he had sent his love this time, she thought, folding the letter to slip over her heart beneath her bra. What was it he had started the note with in that flowing Arabic script? She would have to wait until she saw him; she couldn't ask Raschid. It was Tuesday morning now. Only tomorrow and then Thursday morning to get through.

Brought to her door before breakfast the next morning by a brisk knock upon it, Alex confronted a small, plump, uniformed woman. She had no need to ask why she was there—nurse's dress appears the same in all countries.

'I was told to come to you, Miss Pembroke. Here are the papers with which Mr Yusef has provided me. My name is Ghabah, Nurse Ghabah.' A large brown manilla envelope was proffered.

Brushing it aside, Alex told her, 'It's not necessary to give this to me. I'm sure if Mr Yusef is satisfied, Miss Maitland will be. I'll take you in to the baby now, and you can check what you'll need for the flight, and for the rest of the time we're here. The other nurse is being flown back to Luxor this afternoon.'

# CHAPTER TEN

'But I don't want to go.' Almost sullenly, totally unlike her normal demeanour, Alex answered.

'I don't think we should either, Aunt Elizabeth.' Raschid's voice sounded as unhappy as he looked.

'I've never heard such tommyrot!' The third voice was trenchant. 'Why not, for heaven's sake? I've gone to untold trouble to get a reservation for you— and look at you both!' Miss Maitland was almost as angry as Alex was sullen. 'Just tell me what's the matter with this place, that neither of you wants to go?'

'How did you manage to get a table, Aunt Elizabeth? This nightclub is booked ahead for weeks. I know how impossible it is to go just on the offchance and expect to get in,' asked Raschid carefully.

'Oh, I managed.' A little chuckle accompanied the words, but to the young man whose gaze still rested expectantly upon her, she said snappishly.

'If you must know, Raschid, I went down to the desk—thinking, I might add, that I was providing Alexandra with a treat, because we go straight through Athens on the way home, and she won't get to see the Acropolis.' She raised a hand as Alex tried to interrupt, overriding her voice with a louder one. 'I asked that nice man at the desk to get me a reservation at the top Egyptian night-club in Cairo. He told me he couldn't manage one at . . . at whatever this place is, but could get me a table at the Hilton which had a top European entertainer playing there just now, I informed him in no uncertain manner that I didn't want European entertainment. We were in Cairo and I wanted home-grown stuff.'

'You didn't speak to him like that, I hope? And knowing you, Miss Maitland, you only wanted this place because he said you couldn't have it. . . .'

'Anyway,' again she was overridden, 'I sat there, and he stood there . . . a stand-off. Finally he said, "I really don't think you would like it, Miss Maitland. This other would suit you so much more." It's not what will suit me! You don't think at my age I'm about to go gallivanting around night-clubs? It's for my companion and my nephew,' I told him.

'"Is it Miss Pembroke who wants this reservation?"

"It's for her that I'm making it. Yes!"

"Just a moment, I will see," he said, going to the phone. He was writing on the back on one of the hotel's cards in no time at all. It's over there in my purse—don't forget to take it, or you won't get in.' Miss Maitland glanced from one to the other with that bright malicious smile that was so much a part of her, as much as to say. Look how clever I've been!

Alex didn't think she had been. She shuddered inside at the thought of what Kasseem would say at her going gallivanting—the word was Miss Maitland's, but how apt it was to describe what she would be doing—out to a night-club with another man, an Egyptian to boot, even if that man was Raschid, whom Alex looked upon as an appendage of Miss Maitland's.

So now she gazed across at the expectant face and making the best of it, told her, 'You've been much too good to me already. We will go, though, won't we Raschid, and enjoy ourselves.'

'That's more like it, Alexandra!. Off you go now, and dress up, then come back to be inspected, mind. Just a minute Raschid. . . .'

In her room two doors down, Alex leaned back against the hard wood. Could they not go, and just have dinner somewhere quietly? But that would be worse. Just going to an ordinary hotel or restaurant for a meal when they were staying at a perfectly good hotel in which to have it—at least, at a night-club, they could be going to be entertained as tourists do. Bother! Damn Miss Maitland and her generous gifts!

Oh well, she could be making a mountain out of a molehill. Kasseem mightn't even mind. She wondered if Raschid minded; he hadn't wanted to go.

Shrugging, she set about finding a dress to wear. There was only the necessity of making the choice between two, and she knew which one of them she couldn't wear. Actually, it was a cocktail dress, calf-length, and quite lovely. But it was strapless, and even when she had bought it, Alex had considered it too low-cut across the bustline.

Moving it aside, she withdrew the other that was still packed away and unworn on this trip. This was as different from the cocktail creation as two dresses could be. Fine lilac chiffon drifted about her even as she shook it out. There were no creases, she decided; it didn't need ironing. She laid it across her own bed, then turned down Yasmin's before going to collect her from the nurse.

Alex fastened the tiny pyjama coat, pulling the dressing gown tight. Beginning to brush the curly mop of black hair, she found two small arms reach up to clasp her neck. 'I do like you, Aunty Alex, but I do miss my mummy.'

She caught the small form and hugged it close. 'I know, love. However, soon you'll be in your mummy's home and have all the toys and things that she used to play with. You'll like being there, I promise you. Now, off to Nurse.' Alex waited until she had been admitted to the next room, then closed her door.

Sighing, knowing she couldn't plead a headache and get out of this outing, she realised she had better make a start at getting ready. The reservation was for seven-thirty, and it was seven now. But no one was early for these sort of things.

Showered and perfumed, making up her face before the mirror, Alex used purple eye-shadow, smoothed a pencil over the dark arched eyebrows, then lightly applied a pinkish-purple lipstick. Allowing the folds of chiffon to slide over her shoulders, she pulled up the zip, then fastening the close-fitting wrist cuffs with their tiny pearl buttons, she swung round to look over the whole. High-necked with a myriad pintucks, accompanied by the fragile lilac voluminous sleeves, it could be classed as nothing less than modest even in this country.

Alex clasped the narrow silver belt and pulled it tight, then combing her hair, she fastened it back with the cyclamen combs. They were certainly doing overtime on this trip! Then catching up her purse, she walked the few yards to show herself as she had been ordered.

'You look very well.' Praise indeed from that

source! 'Raschid will be a little late, Alexandra. Ali,
from Old Yusef's, has held him up.'

Alex glanced at her watch—at Kasseem's watch.
They were late already. However, what did she care?
The quicker tonight was over, the better she would
be pleased.

'Oh, I nearly forgot,' added Miss Maitland. 'Get
that card they gave me. It's there on that little
table.'

Turning it over and scrutinising the Arabic script
on the other side of the Shepheards Hotel sign, Alex
wondered what it said, before placing it in her evening bag.

Raschid arrived in a hurry. He gave Alex an old-
fashioned bow, smiled and said, 'You look charming,
Alex. I've kept the car, so you won't have to walk in
that dress.'

Sitting in the back seat, seeing only the driver's
silhouette through the glass partition, Alex looked
out at an unfamiliar night-time city. She started from
her thoughts as Raschid addressed her.

'Sorry, Raschid. I was dreaming. What was it you
said?'

'I asked for that card which has our reservations.
I can't believe we got them for this particular night-
club at such short notice.'

'Oh, sorry again, Raschid.' Alex fumbled in her
purse for the piece of pasteboard. Finally finding it
in the darkness of the car's interior, she handed it
over.

Holding it every way, trying to decipher it in the
passing brightness of lights that came and went,
Raschid gave vent to an exclamation of annoyance,
and reached above to switch on the overhead light.
He read it once, and Alex saw the frown as his glance

scanned it a second time. He reached out again this time, to lower the glass partition and touch the driver on the shoulder, speaking quickly in their own language, then slipping back, he flicked out the light in passing.

'What was all that about, Raschid?'

'It was to tell him to drive around until I tell him to take us on to the night-club.'

'But we're already late!' Alex was moved to protest.

'And we're going to be later still, or not go at all, unless I find out how you're mixed up with the Omair.'

Aghast, stammering at the unexpectedness of having this sharp, almost angry question, thrown at her, Alex queried, 'What ... what do you mean?'

'You are quite an intelligent young woman, Alex. I am sure you can understand a quite simple question.' Alex was astounded, not only because of this subject that was coming at her from out of the blue, but at the manner of the hitherto gentle Raschid.

'How are you involved with the Omair, Alex?' The same question came again. 'I wondered about it in Luxor. I simply couldn't understand how Mohammed happened to be with you, and to be carrying your bag. It was inconceivable. Mohammed is a trusted part of the Sheikh Ahmed ben Omair's Luxor household.'

'Ahmed?' she queried.

'Not the young one from the desert. The Sheikh Kasseem's father is also called Ahmed. I know them, Alex. They live not very far from us. They, of course, are very much more important than my family. But contrary to what Aunt Elizabeth might have thought, we are quite respectable land-holders. I

have known the Sheikh Kasseem, his brother and
two sisters since we were all born. Mohammed was
sent into the desert to be both bodyguard and servant
to Kasseem, who was despatched there at his grandfather's bidding when only a few years old. He just
wouldn't be carrying anyone's bag—unless under
orders.

'Now,' he tapped the card, 'this turns up. Do you
know what is written on it?'

'No.' The one word wasn't uttered in Alex's
normal tone, either. It held breathlessness and right-
eous anger mixed. 'But,' her voice hardened, 'I don't
know how it could be connected with the Omair.
It's just a reservation that a desk clerk got for Miss
Maitland.'

'No desk clerk could get a reservation at this place,
at an hour's notice. It is the most popular and ex-
clusive night-club in Cairo. It says here,' again he
tapped the Arabic script flowing across the card, 'this
is Miss Pembroke, table number twenty-six. By
courtesy of the Omair—not any special member of
that tribe, just by courtesy of the Omair. Do you
know what that implies, Alex? No, of course you
don't, but I do!

'Have you got mixed up with the young Sheikh
Ahmed? Although I don't know him as I do his cous-
ins, I do know his reputation—and he is a person
you definitely shouldn't be involved with. Because
he is who he is, and will one day rule the whole of
the Omair. . . .'

Interrupted violently, he stopped short. 'I'm sick
and tired of hearing the damned name of Omair!'
Alex's voice went high. 'Anyone would think they're
omnipotent! They're not the Sultans of Baghdad
holding the power of olden times. Anyway, the only

involvement I've had with Ahmed was of one solitary meeting. It's Kasseem. . . .'

She got no farther. 'Kasseem? That is not to be believed, Alex. He has nothing to do with foreigners—that is well known.'

'I hate to contradict you, Raschid. However, it is Kasseem I know—in fact, with whom I'm head over heels in love. So there!' As she ended with these two words, she knew how childish they sounded, but she didn't care.

'In love with. . . .' Anger didn't sound in Raschid's voice, but bewilderment did. 'Alex, you can't be! Has he . . . have you . . .?' The words trailed off.

'No, he hasn't, and no, I haven't, but that's only because of his decision, not mine.' She wanted to add again the, 'So there!' But instead she held out a hand entreatingly. 'Raschid, you should understand. You loved Norma; you had obstacles that had to be surmounted.'

'I did, but I was an ordinary middle-class Egyptian. And Kasseem is the eldest son of the Sheikh Ahmed ben Omair of Luxor—a multi-millionaire's son, Alex! And suppose that could be disregarded? There remains the desert Omair. They would never accept it.'

'Kasseem's mother isn't an Arab. His father married an Englishwoman,' Alex protested.

'He did—and look what came of it!'

'It won't turn out like that with me. I love Egypt—maybe not all of it, I suppose, but who loves everything about the country they live in—and Raschid, at the very heart of the matter is the fact that I love Kasseem.'

'But does he love you? Enough to marry you, and take the chance?'

'We'll just have to find out, won't we?' Flippancy
had come defiantly to take over, as continuing, she
said, 'O.K., Raschid, tell the driver we're on our
way. We'll go to this wretched night-club and see if
it's the Omair name that gets us in.'

'Very well, we'll go, Alex, although I would much
rather not be involved in this at all.' Raschid leaned
forward to give the instructions.

Walking through the entrance of this building that
had been discussed so much, Alex wasn't impressed.
She stood just inside the foyer, Raschid behind her
after conferring with the driver of their transport.
'I've told him to collect us at ten. It's eight now;
that gives us two hours.' His tone implied that that
would be more than enough.

Inside, she was impressed. It was magnificent, and
so different from anything she had ever seen at home;
Eastern in every respect. However, she glanced
quickly around, amazed. It was barely half full.
Almost a whole side was empty, although most of
the tables around the one to which they were led
held diners. Their card had been accepted by a dig-
nified elderly Egyptian in native dress, who had
showed no sign whatsoever that it held any interest
out of the ordinary.

They were placed by one of the tall pillars that
ran in a double line down the centre of the night-
club, and were hardly seated when there was stir
and bustle sending a vibration across the entire
room. Music made itself heard, softly at first, unfamiliar, but taking on an insistent rhythm.

Through the entrance came a procession, the sight
of which caused Alex to sit rigid in her seat. Good
heavens! She hadn't expected this. Kasseem had said
his family were entertaining guests, but she hadn't

expected it to be in a place where any member of
the public would have access. But would any of the
public have had that access? She and Raschid would
not have been given a table, except for Miss
Maitland's intimation that it was Alex who was
making the booking. Heavens, did all Egypt know
about her?

Damn Miss Maitland! What had possessed her, to
want to send Alex out on a night on the town on this
of all nights? And damn, too, that clerk at
Shepheards. He need not even have mentioned this
place.

All the time these thoughts were tumbling through
her mind, Alex's gaze, intense, concentrated, was on
the leading figure. Kasseem was dressed as she had
first seen him at the airport, but over the immaculate
white was a robe of black threaded with silver, which
ran shimmering against darkness as he moved.

The older man he was escorting so deferentially
showed a bearded face, a composure that took defer-
ence as his right. They were sitting, each as they
had filed in, around a long, low table; not individual
small ones, Alex noticed. Farther along from
Kasseem and the man he had been escorting was a
much younger Arab, and she saw the familiar twist of
black and silver cord about his head. Before she
could even ask about it from Raschid, her gaze was
caught by a look being directed deliberately across
the room at her.

The glance was from Ahmed, a curious smile tight
at the corner of his lips. The barest inclination of his
head followed. 'Damn him too!' she muttered to
herself. She might as well include everything and
everybody in her imprecations. How had he ever
managed to notice her when his whole attention

should have been on the important gathering around him?

Abruptly, unexpectedly, inside her came a tension of warning; her gaze skimmed over the men between Ahmed and the tall man who was listening with bent head to the comments his guest was making. Kasseem's head might have been courteously lowered, but he was looking across at her, taking in both her presence there, and her companion. 'And damn you too, Kasseem,' she muttered under her breath. It was true what they said about the Omair. How could both he and Ahmed possibly have seen her among the flow of people and waiters all around? Raschid was practically hidden by the large pillar, and they were not in the front row of tables at all.

However, there was no inclination of the head from this second glance that had found her. He wasn't pleased, Alex knew, even while thinking how stupid she was to believe that displeasure could possibly reach out across this noisy crowded room.

The glance was broken. A troupe of entertainers had bounded in, their brilliant colours and contortions separating them. Their dinner, which Raschid had ordered without consulting Alex, was being served. All he wanted to do, she knew without being told, was to dine and go.

Eating food that at another time, another place, she would have enjoyed because of its strangeness, she kept her eyes on her plate, but her attention on that long table ablaze with noise and laughter. This was no diplomatic formal dinner; it looked like a celebration. She hoped Kasseem was celebrating too. . . . And the deviousness he had said he was practising, and the surprises he had planned for somebody, had been as successful as he had hoped—whatever they were.

It might not have been a diplomatic dinner; it might have been organised for pleasure and enjoyment. But Alex noted, even so, that a white-clad bearded Arab stood directly behind Kasseem's principal guest. Her gaze, roving farther, saw that two others also had attendants behind them—and so had Kasseem, and Ahmed, but not the young Arab on the father's side.

'Who is the young man on the other side of Kasseem's guest?' she asked, when a waiter had served them another course, and departed.

Without even bothering to turn around and look, Raschid replied, 'The Prince is between Kasseem and his brother Khalid.'

'Oh.' Her attention aroused, Alex's glance was more intent. Quite a bit younger than Kasseem, she thought, and not a scrap like him. Strange that, when Kasseem and his second cousin showed such flashes of similarity.

She mentioned this fact. 'Yes,' answered her companion, 'Khalid is more like his Saudi relations. His mother comes from there, I expect you knew. Some of these nobles here tonight would probably be connections of his.' Raschid went on placidly eating his dinner, giving no attention whatever to the goings-on at that noisy, exuberant table, seen very clearly now that the entertainers had finished their routine and vanished.

'Khalid? Does he live at Luxor? He's never been mentioned. And why hasn't he got a bodyguard behind him too?' asked Alex.

'Although his father is an Omair, Khalid is not classed as one. He is a politician here in Cairo, and

a very able one too, I'm told, but not important
enough to warrant a bodyguard. It's the Omair
behind Ahmed and Kasseem. Of course, Alex, there
is no necessity for them to be there— it is only a
matter of prestige. Tonight this entire place will be
guarded. The army will be at every door and opening. Egypt wouldn't risk, in the slightest degree,
anything happening to these guests—which is the
reason we are leaving at ten o'clock sharp. You
wouldn't want to stay, anyhow. It is going to get
considerably wilder as the night progresses.'

This Alex could well believe. It was beginning to
get that way now. Then abruptly, almost eerily, a
complete silence had fallen. Lights went lower and
the drums began. Raschid had turned in his chair
for the first time, looking not at the long table, but
at a cleared space in front of it.

Into this, gliding, came a woman—no, only a girl.
Beautiful ... oh, yes, even breathtaking, thought
Alex, who wasn't easily swayed by women's looks.
In shimmering gauze that hid nothing of a figure
that it only sparsely covered, she halted her glide in
front of the older guest between the two brothers,
and slowly, sensually, began to dance.

The drums weren't loud, but their beat sent an
anticipation through the senses. Alex felt it herself,
and she was no Arab. She couldn't take her gaze off
that twirling form which gave to every movement,
every twist, every gyration, the promise of what her
body was performing. Alex found her own blood
mounting, excitement closing her throat tight. She
shook her head to clear it, her glance travelling
round the blue-hazed room. She was no Egyptian
man, to be mesmerised by an art honed to perfection
over the centuries since time immemorial.

In all that crowded room, one person's attention wasn't on that gyrating dancer's movements. Across it, Alex gazed into green eyes, and her throat really did go dry now. For a full minute that look held, then was broken as the dancer bent over backwards, head almost on the floor, her body sheened with perpiration, opened and exposed before the man Raschid had called the Prince.

He leaned over, a hand outstretched. Clapping and stamping echoed around the large room, as from Kasseem's hand, not the Prince's, came the clink and flash of yellow. Bringing herself upright with a little twisted jump, the dancer made a low obeisance before him. She gathered up what he had given her, and with another sinking to the floor, ran down the room.

'That's it, Alex.' Raschid was on his feet, a waiter beckoned to his side. The room was jumping, men were clapping the dancer back.

Alex picked up her purse and watched as Raschid placed money on the paper he had been handed. Then without a backward glance, they left a room that was just beginning the night's entertainment.

## CHAPTER ELEVEN

ALEX was brushing Yasmin's curls, tidying her after breakfast, when their door crashed open, and startled, they both turned. Alex was the more alarmed to see that it was Miss Maitland who had caused the commotion, Raschid hovering unhappily in the background behind her as she entered. Alex had risen with only one thought in her mind this morning: it was Thursday, and Kasseem's note had said he would see her some time.

Even this was pushed from her mind now as she dropped the brush and hurried forward. Catching one of the frail outstretched arms, she remarked calmly, gently, 'Sit down, Miss Maitland. What's upset you?'

'That Old Yusef! Look what he's sent me!' Alex glanced at the large piece of foolscap fluttering from her hand.

'But, Aunt Elizabeth. . . .' Raschid stopped, as his aunt waved him to silence.

'Now really, Miss Maitland!' Alex had never used this tone before. 'You're frightening Yasmin. Calm down!'

'It's Mr Yusef's bill. I realise it's large—but, Alex, he's had a great deal of work to do.' Now that Miss Maitland had subsided, Raschid got his words in.

'Does it matter, Miss Maitland? He has been in evidence a lot,' Alex pointed out.

'No, I don't suppose it matters, but it is exorbitant. Just look!' Alex looked and almost turned white. She gazed across to Rachid.

'My aunt,' he answered her look, 'wants us to leave Egypt as soon as possible. Mr Yusef has accomplished this, and we are booked to leave on tomorrow's plane. I don't like to have to say it, but it does take money here to get bureaucracy moving quickly, to get visas and passports processed. If it is too much, maybe my family can help with it.'

He couldn't have said anything more to the point to bring calmness into the room. 'What nonsense, Raschid!' the old lady told him. 'It's not the money;

it's just Old Yusef thinking he can line his pockets for his old age at my expense.'

Alex laughed, right out loud, and the tension evaporated. 'You're incorrigible, Miss Maitland,' she said. 'Just because it's. . . .' She pulled herself up abruptly. She had nearly said Old Yusef herself. '—Mr Yusef. Is it really exorbitant, Raschid?'

'I don't honestly think so. I will grant you it is not cheap, but he did save you money on that land deal, Aunt Elizabeth. You would have paid a lot more but for him—I think it works even.'

'There! Count your blessings, Miss Maitland, and tell us what's doing today.' Alex didn't say, are we really leaving Egypt tomorrow? She didn't want to actually say the words. She wouldn't even think about it until she had seen Kasseem.

'I'm going off to the robber baron's office to pay this account and finalise every least little thing that needs finalising,' announced Miss Maitland. 'And, as he had got us away sooner than I expected, I might even take him to lunch. There, Alexandra, that's magnanimity for you, so don't Miss Maitland me in that tone! As for you, you're going with Raschid to pick up those plaques I ordered. I'll drop you off on my way. You can get a taxi back here, then use it to go any place you haven't yet seen. Go and take some more snaps of the Sphinx. You spoilt your last lot while we were at the Pyramids, didn't you? We'll have dinner here together, all of us, the nurse and Yasmin too, as a family. And then tomorrow—home. Thank God!'

'Not me,' muttered Alex very softly. 'I'm not giving any thanks yet.'

They collected the two large cardboard-crated plaques, executed in copper and beaten silver, which

her companion had ordered specially made. She had
wanted them finished in finer detail and with better
quality silver than those mass-produced for the tourist trade. Alex thought them beautiful.

'The Nefertiti head is for Yasmin,' said Raschid,
seeing her appreciation of them. 'The barge with
Pharaoh sailing to Thebes is for Raschid Peter. It
was a nice gesture on Aunt Elizabeth's part, wasn't
it? A daily reminder of their heritage. I really
wouldn't have expected it of her.'

'No, nor would I,' answered Alex. 'It only goes to
show you, doesn't it?' She went on in a lighter tone,
'Raschid Peter—is that the baby's name? Much to
my disgrace, I've always called him the baby. I
probably knew he had a name, but in all the wheel-
ing and dealing, I didn't think to enquire.' More
hesitantly, she asked, 'Is he . . . has he been christened? She knew Raschid would be a Muslim. But if
Yasmin and the baby were too, she had no idea.

'Yes, in both religions. Not with a big splash, you
understand, but Norma wanted it that way. My
parents didn't object. They expected that living in
Egypt it would right itself in time. I'm not a fanatic,
Alex. We'll see what the Lord or Allah brings.'

'I think a lot more of us should have such ideas,
Raschid,' she told him, while wondering about her
own case. What ideas, or ideals, did Kasseem hold?
Had he been christened in both faiths? How would
she. . . . She shrugged. Like Raschid, she would see
what the Lord or Allah brought.

'What do you call him—the baby?' she asked now,
as they left the shop, each lumbered with an enormous square package.

Raschid laughed—the first time, thought Alex in
astonishment, she had heard a laugh from this serious

young man. 'We have arrived at a compromise, Aunt Elizabeth and I. She and her friends are to call him Peter, Yasmin and I will call him Raschid. What do you think of that, Alex?'

'That I'll give him both names, and call him Raschid Peter, whenever I see him.' If I do see him, she added under her breath.

Raschid produced a warm smile and looked down at her. 'You are a nice person, Alex,' he said.

As she turned to meet that smile, her foot kicked against an upthrust piece of cement on the paving. The unwieldy, very large parcel knocked against her other leg, and she was almost over into the gutter. Endeavouring to prevent her falling, obstructed by his own package, Raschid grabbed her with his free arm, bringing her body upright against his own.

For a minute she remained there, trying to regain her balance. Then resting the awkward, bulky plaque against her leg, she stood upright unaided, and turned to the man holding her. 'Thank you, Raschid. I was nearly a goner into that gutter!'

'Yes, you were.' The dark pleasant face looked down upon her, only anxiety for her welfare showing, nothing else. She could have been Nurse Ghabah he had saved from falling.

He eased down his own plaque carefully and then released her. 'All right now?' he asked. 'That footpath should be mended. Anyone could get badly hurt stumbling over it.' He kicked at the offending protuberance.

'Yes, I am now. But, Raschid, let's put these wretched things in a taxi and send them to the hotel—they're too much of a handful to be carrying around. Then we'll go back to the Pyramids as your aunt suggested, and I'll get my shots of that incredible Sphinx.' She was looking up at him, smiling.

Neither of them noticed a long black car in the
endless stream of traffic that had moved slowly along
towards, opposite, and then past them. They did not
see, either, the two white-clad men sitting in its back
seat, and had not seen the one whose gaze had
alighted upon them at the very moment Raschid
had clasped her to him, noticing that she remained
there, smiling up at the man holding her. Again,
neither of them saw the head swivel backwards as
the limousine passed, to observe them both still
embraced, one gazing down, the other up, smiling.

The kaffiyeh-covered head with its twisted black
and silver cord bent courteously as a comment came
from his companion, but Alex would not have
recognised this face. Every line appeared changed,
giving the countenance a ruthlessness that made
Ahmed's boyish in comparison. Beneath half-shut
eyes showed a look that dredged back an era old a
thousand years ago; exposing a cruelty that desert
tribesmen had practised as their natural right.

However, no foreboding came to spoil the happy
morning that followed for Alex. The plaques were
despatched to the hotel, and another taxi took them
to the Pyramids. Alex stood gazing at them. They
*were* incredible, when you actually took them in—
rearing to the vivid blue of the sky, blotting out the
landscape with their bulk. Not something that nature
had created, but that man had. Like the millions
before her who had stood where she was now standing, she wondered how.

She had not liked crawling behind the guides
through the passages towards the hollowed-out
rooms. These were different from those of the Valley
of the Kings. At least, there, they were only a little

way inside the earth. These she didn't like at all. But it had been different altogether when she had first laid eyes on the Sphinx crouching there on the desert floor. An instant love affair had been born.

So now, standing beside Raschid, she took her snaps and fell in love all over again with the half beast, half woman, lying there, so magnificent, so indifferent to the crowds milling all around.

They had lunch at the open-air café with its outline brooding over them, but, suddenly restless, in case Mustafa called when she was away, Alex told Raschid she had had enough sightseeing. A perfectly valid excuse was available, for cases did need to be sorted and packed—not only her own, but Yasmin's and Miss Maitland's as well. And heaven knew how the last two were to be managed.

They had their family dinner, Yasmin and the baby too, in the dining room. Saying goodnight to Miss Maitland at the door of her room, with Yasmin, Alex proceeded to her own to undress and put her to bed, butterflies working overtime beneath her diaphragm. They had become more acute as the day and then the evening wore on. Preparing for the night, Alex played the usual games with the little girl, then she tucked her into bed, and told her more curtly then was normal to go to sleep. The overhead light off, Alex settled down with a book, using only her bedside lamp for illumination. She might have had a book in her hand, and she might have been looking at the printed page, but no meaning of the words penetrated.

Asleep, Yasmin's even breathing caused her to bring up her wrist. Ten-thirty! Surely Mustafa would come soon. Almost sick with anticipation and the growing tension throughout the long day, Alex was finding it difficult to think clearly. All she wanted was Kasseem's presence and she knew everything would fall into place.

The knock was so soft, she almost didn't hear it. When it was repeated, the book fell from her suddenly nerveless hands to the floor, and she was off the bed, moving quickly to the door. The figure in the aperture as it opened was no Mustafa, however; it was Ahmed.

'Good evening, Alex,' he said. 'I have been sent to escort you. Do you ride?'

Silent, Alex stood there, endeavouring to adjust to Ahmed when she had expected Mustafa. 'Ride?' she queried. 'What do you mean, Ahmed?'

'Have you ever ridden a horse?' Baldly, he repeated the query.

'Yes . . . at least. . . .' Suddenly a memory flashed before her inside vision. 'Yes,' her voice went high, 'I *have* ridden, quiet horses for a pleasant afternoon's amble. There's no way, however, I'd get on one of those animals that I saw in Luxor. No way!' she repeated.

The smile that she knew came to soften those hard lips. 'You will be able to manage the one you'll be mounted upon. You don't imagine I would risk my skin by having you hurt yourself, do you? Now, put this on.'

'This', was a long white robe with a hood. Alex looked askance towards it, but allowed it to be dropped round her shoulders, strings pulled tight and fastened across her chest.

'Come along,' said Ahmed, and detained her as she made to re-enter the room, muttering about her handbag. 'Leave it,' he told her.

She swung round on him, the long white robe

swirling about her feet. With the hood pulled around her face, she wouldn't be recognised. She wondered if that was what it was all about. She protested, 'But it's got my passport and money in it, Ahmed. It didn't matter in Luxor—they were all in the hotel safe. We have them now, ready for tomorrow.'

'Alex,' his patience was thinly veiled, 'leave them. Nothing will happen to them—the floor porter knows who I am. No stranger would be allowed near your room. Come, we are wasting time.'

Spoken to in that tone, she went, and it was the man who reached round and shut the door. They passed the corridor station unseen as far as Alex could make out. No one looked at them as they bypassed the main lifts. They were received into a ground floor hallway, from where it took only a few steps to the outside. Ushered into the rear of a black limousine, Ahmed was beside her, his servant in front beside the driver.

'Where are we going, Ahmed?' she wanted to know.

'Oh,' his tone had changed now from peremptory ordering to almost complacency, 'having received instructions to collect and transport you to a place of privacy, I decided to let you see how I live. Would you like that, Alex?'

Underneath the laughing words, some other nuance surfaced, one she couldn't fathom. This wasn't the open Ahmed with whom she had talked when he had taken her home to the Winter Palace hotel.

'Yes,' she answered, but there was reserve in her tone, 'but where are we going?'

'Out in the desert.' At that, she turned from him to glance out of her wide window. They had left the city behind and over to the left in the darkness could be discerned the bulk of the Pyramids. Ahmed remained silent, but that state didn't last long. In ten minutes or less, the rushing sound of quick progress through the night slowed.

Pulling off on to the shoulder of a road that had changed from bitumen to pot-holed gravel, they were surrounded by a group of bearded horsemen. There was no greeting, no answering talk. Ahmed led Alex to one of the spare mounts waiting. She glanced from it to him, and in the darkness saw the gleam of white. He was smiling.

'You'll be quite safe, Alex,' his voice said. 'Here,' he bent down, cupping his hands. She took hold of the reins, put her foot into the step provided for her, and lightly jumped. She was in the saddle, her feet in the stirrups, her cloak arranged about her—and the little horse still stood quietly. It gave her confidence. Then Ahmed spoke in Arabic, and suddenly she was trotting.

The desert was all around them; only the sound of thudding hooves cushioned by the sand on which they struck, and the creak of saddle leather, broke the hush in which they moved. The horses quickened into an easy canter; and handling her mount with greater confidence, Alex now found she had time to look about her. There was no moon silvering the desert sands tonight. But she had been lucky; she had seen the Nile sheened with its brilliance on two occasions, an image that would never be eradicated.

Still, even if there was no moon, a luminosity showed the shapes of the riders grouped about her, and glancing upwards, she saw the stars, scintillating like diamonds that had been scattered by a lavish band. It was their brilliance that provided the faint brightness. Alex drew a deep breath. It was ex-

hilarating to be riding through the vast silence, the
breeze blowing against her swiftly moving figure,
and quite cool, she noticed in astonishment. She had
never been cold all the time she had been in Egypt.

Something else she noticed—the four Arabs riding
escort were cantering in a semi-circle, two at the
back and one on either side just behind Ahmed and
his own young Arab. For the entire journey, the
exact distance was maintained. It was like watching
precision flying, and must have taken the same
gruelling practice.

They seemed to be riding on for ever. Feeling
tiredness starting to overwhelm her, Alex began to
wonder if they would ever arrive at wherever they
were going. Then, in the faint starshine, a smudge
on the horizon came to mar the emptiness about
them. And, so suddenly she almost thought she had
imagined it, there came a blink of light. Could it be
a star so low down? But just then another, brighter
light showed, and in a few minutes they were among
movement—men, fidgeting horses, and the civilisation of tents. And in profusion, palm trees rose to
meet the heavens, high and rustling in the night
breeze.

Ahmed was beside her mount. He held her stirrup
and she swung down. She stood a moment, regaining
her equilibrium, a hand resting on the little horse
that had carried her so effortlessly. A fire, blazing
some yards away, outlined a cluster of tents. Farther
to the right stood a larger erection, and towards that,
Ahmed indicated they should go.

He reached down and an opening appeared in
the canvas side. Going through it, Alex stood just
inside, gazing about her. Austere could have been
used for this outer annex. A carpet covered the floor

upon which she stood. Chairs, some low tables, and a very large carved chest completed the furnishings. But there was a tent within a tent, and, at a further indication from Ahmed, she walked towards an opening of this second shelter outlined by lights from within.

A gasp escaped from her open lips. Had it deliberately been arranged and furnished like a film set from an Arabian Nights picture? She swung round on her companion. 'What is this, Ahmed? Why the long journey? Where is Kasseem?'

'Kasseem will be here in a short while. He hasn't been able to get away before now. And at this late hour there is no place he could see you. His launch is still at Luxor, and he stays at Khalid's house. As to what this is—it is the accommodation arranged for me when I am travelling.'

'You mean you actually use something like this all the time?' Abruptly she paused. She hadn't really meant the words to sound as they had done. Ahmed's face was suddenly not that of a friendly young man's, but that of a desert chieftain who knows his place—and his power. His eyebrows had a deep cleft between them, and that mouth she had always thought ruthless was just that.

'Yes, I do mean that! I travel a great deal, and I am going to be doing so for a number of years yet, so I expect to be comfortable. My men also have that same expectation. We are the Omair, after all, not rootless *fellahin*. But should you think the place has been used; it hasn't. I too stay at Khalid's palace. This,' an outflung arm encompassed the whole softly-lit room, 'has only been set up in case. The oasis belongs to us, you know.'

'I'm sorry, Ahmed. It's just that it took my breath

away,' she told him. And it had! The hanging walls were woven of some blue shimmering material, caught up high in the centre of the ceiling. A carpet covered the sand, but it was nothing like the outside one. It looked as one would imagine a Persian carpet to look, and knowing how Ahmed thought, it probably was.

There was two low tables, inlaid with ivory, one holding what appeared to be an antique coffee pot with two small cups. However, the pièce de résistance was the couch/bed. It was a flat couch with only an uprising headrest, and no sides, set upon four golden lions' feet. Piled high upon it were cushions.

The magnetic colours blazed, giving a total impression of luxury; yet through it all was the suggestion of being there for use, providing only the necessities for living. Every piece of furniture was in its place, and every place was for a practical purpose.

'I will leave you, Alex. I have things to attend to. Kasseem will be here in due time. There is coffee there, if you feel like it.' Before she could reply, Ahmed had departed through the hooked-up aperture, and passed beyond the outer canvas walls.

There was coffee—hot too, she saw, pausing in her prowling back and forth. It was a thick Turkish brew, however, and she shuddered away from it. Suddenly she realised how little she had eaten today—that lunch out at the Pyramid restaurant, where she had hardly touched anything, and at dinner tonight she had been too keyed up. Even so, she wasn't hungry. Oh, how she wished Kasseem would come!

Back and forth again she prowled. She glanced down at her high-heeled sandals sinking into the soft carpet. Tonight she had dressed up for dinner, something she had not done on this trip, except in the grey dress Kasseem had brought for her, when they went to the Karnak temple, and of course to the night-club in a long formal dress. Not knowing who would actually be calling for her, she had dressed in a lemon crêpe-de-chine blouse, with a swirling silk skirt of lemon that matched it. The colour suited her, more here than in Australia, lighting up her apricot skin and darkening her grey eyes.

A glance at her watch showed after one o'clock. She had been waiting for more than half an hour. Purposefully she stalked through to the outer tent, restless, thinking that to wait outside in the fresh desert air might help pass the time.

She lifted the flap, but as she moved to stand in the opening, a figure stood before it. It was in Arabic that he spoke, and softly too. But the message was perfectly clear. She was to return inside.

Damn Ahmed!—but there was nothing else to do. Alex returned inside. Sitting down upon that fantastic couch, she moved one of the cushions, stroking the soft velvet texture. She couldn't remain still, though, and stood up to resume her pacing.

Suddenly her head came up, her glance turning towards the hooked-backed opening. Yes, she *had* heard something. There came the sound of horses, the bustle of an arrival. There was talk too, back and forth in Arabic, and one of the voices was from the man for whom she was waiting.

A quick muffled step on the outside carpet sounded, and abruptly the aperture was filled. Alex started to run across to him, calling his name then, almost in mid-air, she stopped.

He stood there silently, then flung the riding whip he had been carrying on to one of the small tables. Unaware that she had even noticed, Alex knew that it had rolled off and dropped to the floor.

In the doorway, the man reached up to unhook the blue silk and allowed it to fall, closing the small room.


# CHAPTER TWELVE

'KASSEEM!' Alex's hand went out. 'What. . . . Is something the matter?' she asked this stranger.

'Should there be? I have only a few hours' leisure and I have come to employ them for the pleasure of us both. On the last two occasions we were interrupted. I can assure you that that will not be the case this time.' As he spoke he was divesting himself of his headdress. The outer robe followed and both were thrown haphazardly on to the second small table.

Alex tried again. 'What's happened, Kasseem? You're . . .' she couldn't bring herself to say 'different'. But this man was a stranger. She looked more closely at the face that was returning her gaze across this luxurious room that was Ahmed's.

Like hers, his words were repeated 'Should there be anything the matter? Should anything have happened? I merely feel like indulging myself with a few hours' lovemaking before I fly out tomorrow. Surely that is understandable to you?'

'You're drunk!' she said flatly.

'Drunk. My dear Alexandra,' softly, like the slither of silk, the words reached her, 'don't you know that we of the Muslim faith are forbidden alcohol?' Then came words from which every sign of softness had entirely disappeared 'I only wish to Allah I were drunk! In that case I could imagine that what I know now was inspired by the wild imagery of intoxication.'

She looked at him, utterly unable to take in the violent words, seeing the green pinpoints of light behind lids that this time were wide open. 'If you're not drunk, you must have been smoking hashish! I want to go home!'

'Do you now, my little houri of promiscuousness? But why? Is not one man like another. If you can stand in broad daylight in the middle of a Cairo street, clamped body to body in a man's passionate embrace, surely in this room prepared for us,' an outflung arm gestured to it all, the silken hangings, the beautiful carpet, that luxurious couch, 'you will enjoy it all the more?'

'But Raschid was. . . .' What could she say? How could she explain to this . . . this Arab that she had only been saved from falling into the gutter? She had no time to even begin to try.

'What was Raschid?'

Ice-cold, her whole body shaking, Alex who interrupted this time. 'You should train your spies more thoroughly! Instruct them to see occurrences from start to finish, and further, to interpret what they do see properly.'

'It wasn't what you call my "spies". If they had witnessed that scandalous embrace, I scarcely think they would have reported it—they would have been too frightened. I saw it for myself, my thanks to

Allah. And the interpretation was there for anyone to read. There was no withdrawal. You were happy to be in his arms. You were smiling up at him. You had your hand upon his shoulder—for the entire population of Cairo to watch and enjoy.' One after another followed the accusations.

'But,' now the violence had died, and silken words took their place, 'why should such behaviour surprise me? You showed me yourself what it was like, the very first time you met me when you lay naked in my arms.'

Red-hot anger had come to replace the icy shaking, and Alex's reply came from between clenched teeth, but so sweetly, showing nothing of the rage behind it. 'Of course, you shouldn't be surprised, Kasseem. But aren't you exaggerating just a little? I didn't offer myself to you at our very first meeting, surely, Wasn't it the second? After all, I couldn't offer all I had to give in a crowded airport, now could I? But in a bedroom on a launch—not perhaps as luxurious as this, but still. . . .'

His face had gone white—no, of course it couldn't go white, not that brown skin, but it had drained to grey as her words hit at him. The lips thinned, and a hand struck fast. It took hold of her shoulder, but as, frightened by that look, she moved back a pace, it slipped upon the fragile crêpe-de-chine.

There came the sound of tearing. The violence of the force he had used to pull her to him had ripped away the three small crystal buttons that fastened it. The blouse lay open and pulled from the skirt.

Vowing inside herself to make no other effort to combat a strength so much more powerful than her own, she stood before him, a lip curled in contempt.

She made no attempt, either, to cover a body which had merely a scrap of nylon lace to cover a nakedness the ripped blouse had left exposed.

Crushed in his hand, the fragile material was used to pull her towards him, and Alex felt his hand, as she had on other occasions, spreadeagle low upon her back, bringing flesh to meet flesh. Her body this time, however, was doing no melting into his. It was rigid, iron-bar straight. Kasseem laughed then, not a happy sound; one coming from deep in his throat. 'You will respond to me, Alexandra, before this night is over.'

Gazing beyond his shoulder, voice tight, she answered, 'I can't stop anything you propose to do. How can I? Against not only you, but against the whole tribe you have out there to help you.' As much contempt as she could manage she put into those words. 'But it will be you alone doing any love-making that occurs. There will be no response from me, I promise you!'

Again he laughed, and again the sound of it frightened her. His lips rested at her temple. She knew the touch of them, but that fact made no difference; it might have been a statue he held in his arms.

Down her throat slowly, so slowly, they travelled, to rest in turn above the two half-moons of lace. Suddenly they had dropped, and had lightly touched the bare sliver of midriff between bra and skirt. A tremor shot through her body—and that hateful laugh came again.

She was swung up and deposited among the cushions, his body outstretched beside her, resting on an imprisoned arm beneath it. The passion and desire he was pouring forth upon her now was slow flowering, mouth merely touching lips that gave no return, resting upon other places that she knew, against her will, jumped at the touch of them.

Deep inside her where there was comprehension, she knew the reason for the slow lovemaking Kasseem was forcing upon her. It was to exact the response so freely given on other occasions. And she knew, also, that he would win. She would be unable not to return caress for caress. But it would not be the response of free will; she would know that, and if Kasseem did, he wouldn't care.

The arm beneath her spreading along her back abruptly pulled her closer, endeavouring to fit curve into curve even more tightly. His other hand stroked from her waist down over the silken hips, then trailed leisurely up again along the body that the skirt was covering. His mouth came seeking urgently, and she knew there would be no stopping for him now. Tears that she had resolutely held back trickled down her cheeks to drop over on to her neck—tears of regret for what could have been. His lips were upon hers again, searching, making no pretence now of asking for co-operation, wanting, demanding, crushing away thought and reason, and then without volition, those bruising caresses were carrying her along with him, regrets, thought, everything, gone with the wind.

Unexpectedly, Kasseem raised his head, one arm still clasping her body stretched tight against him, the other resting below her hips on the silken yellow skirt. It was this one that was lifted to wipe against his mouth.

'Allah . . .!' It was in Arabic, that violent expletive, then Kasseem had risen to stand looking down at her. 'Tears, Alexandra? Somehow I didn't think that of you—to use them as a weapon.'

'I didn't . . . I'm not. I'm not crying.' Half up on an elbow, she gazed back at him from drowned eyes. She hadn't been crying as such, either. The tears had fallen in regret for something beautiful that was lost. 'I'm not crying,' she reiterated.

He had turned away. Hooking back the blue silk hanging, he disappeared, and she heard his voice, curt, sharply giving what sounded like orders.

'Get up and get properly dressed.' His words on his return startled her. Dazedly unable to take in this abrupt new dimension which had shattered the passion encircling them only seconds ago, she swung her feet round to the floor and stared up at him.

'Go home, Alexandra,' he said in that still harsh tone. 'It couldn't have been expected to last. Fairy stories don't happen nowadays!' He bent down to reach for a hand to bring her up from the couch, then swiftly backed, as she shrank away.

'Very well. Just get up and go, and thank your God as I thank Allah that I saw in time the impossibility of a union between us. And I thank Allah, also, that at last I have found that I am an Arab, who acts and thinks as an Arab does. To see the woman I thought of as mine manhandled by any male who chooses to has at least made that clear.'

The words dried the tears on her cheeks, and her glance was as stormy, as full of contempt as his own; but she was shaking, hardly able to stand. She did see, however, that all-encompassing glance that raked over her, and felt the blood mount to a face that had been drained of colour. Her shaking hands went up in an endeavour to make the sliding material of her torn blouse stay together. With buttons ripped off, it was a forlorn hope. She tried stuffing it in the waistband of her skirt and holding the blouse as close together as she was able.

There came the noise of trampling hooves, the jingle of bridle bits. The man picked up the robe that Ahmed had dropped over her in Cairo. He made, however, no attempt to place it round her; he held it out and as she made no move to accept it, dropped it at her feet, and turned away, waiting.

With no alternative, except that of going out before the eyes of the tribesmen in ripped and disarranged clothes, Alex stooped to retrieve the little heap of cloth and dropped it about her shoulders. Her shaking finger couldn't get the strings tied. They were taken from her and fastened, the cloak swished more concealingly around her form, the hood pulled up. Then he was gone and the outside canvas flap opened.

He wouldn't have wanted any of his Arabs to see her like this, she thought acidly, even if he was finished with her. So perforce she followed, pulling the hood even closer. Just as on her outward trip, her escort waited.

Ahmed came to help her, but as his two hands came out, she cringed away: she wanted no one to touch her. Unseen, Ahmed's gaze passed across the back of the little horse to meet that of his cousin's, and his eyebrow went high. Kasseem shook his head.

Alex's still shaking hands had found a stirrup, and awkwardly, with one foot in it, she jumped and pulled herself up on to the patient mount. Ahmed went to speak to that tall, forbidding figure, standing immobile, outlined in relief by the blazing fire behind him. He was waved peremptorily away. As before, on the first night's ride in the desert, there came a command in Arabic and her mount was cantering. Without a backward look she went, her thoughts shying away from the previous hour, her mind numb. What the future would hold at that moment she didn't know, and she didn't care. But Kasseem was right. If he could come to the conclusions he had, merely by seeing Raschid catch her as she almost fell, it wouldn't have worked.

Her horse stumbled and Ahmed's hand came out. She didn't want that; she put her concentration into just riding. There was no upward glancing at the stars. She only wanted to get to the privacy of her own room.

It didn't seem to take so long, this second journey. There suddenly came the sliding halt among men guarding the two limousines. Stiffly Alex began to dismount, and although Ahmed stood at her mount's head, he made no attempt to assist her.

The door of one of the cars was opened, and she climbed inside. Ahmed came to sit beside her, but with yards of upholstery separating them. As the limousine started, he spoke. 'Alex . . .!' She turned away, gazing out of her window, not answering.

'Look, Alex,' Ahmed began again.

'I don't want to talk. I don't want to speak about it. Please leave me alone.' She couldn't bring herself even to say his name.

In only the few minutes it took, they were again at Shepheards, and it was on her side that Ahmed's servant opened the door. 'I can find my own way,' said Alex, as Ahmed went to walk beside her.

A muttered expletive in Arabic sounded. Then in English, in a tone quite as dictatorial as any Kasseem had used, her companion said, 'Don't be stupid, Alex. You don't know this way in, and I have no intention of not seeing you to your room.' He indicated the passage opening up before her, but didn't, as he never had done, she realised, seeing that fact in tonight's context, take her arm to pilot her.

She pulled the enveloping cloak tight about her, the lift swished up and they passed the porter on duty. At her room, she reached for the door knob, intending to leave without a word, but she was prevented. A hand from out of a voluminous white sleeve had grasped it.

'Alex,' said Ahmed, 'you are leaving tomorrow, and I'd like to say goodbye. I am truly sorry it has ended this way between you and my cousin. Why, I simply don't know, but in all my life with him I have never seen him so blazingly angry as he was when he gave the orders to collect you. What in the name of Allah happened?'

Alex shrugged. 'Something only an Arab would take offence at.' For the first time since they had left the oasis and embarked on the homeward journey, she looked directly at him, at the face she had first seen riding in Luxor—stern, the lips compressed and, suddenly, older, not a youth's face any more.

'I just know, Ahmed,' she told him in a slow dragging voice, 'that if our love had been consummated that night on the launch when you interrupted us—whatever came of it, I would have taken home only warmth and happiness with me. Now, when I remember Egypt, the blueness, the warmth and happiness are gone, and only dark despair remains. I want to forget I ever came here.' A half smile appeared on the drawn, strained face, for the briefest moment as she continued.

'I've always been a little afraid of you, Ahmed.'

'Afraid? Of me?' she was interrupted.

'Yes—and don't look at me with that amazed expression. You do all you can to foster that emotion.

Do you know what I said to myself that night in Luxor when you escorted me home? I said, 'Aren't I lucky that I fell in love with Kasseem? Ahmed is the other side of love's coin'. I see now that that applies to Kasseem as well.' Before he could find an answer, she said sadly, 'Goodbye, Ahmed!'

This time she found a bare doorknob and turned it. She moved inside and closed it carefully, then with her back leaning against it, she stared around. It was incredible to find the room exactly as she had left it, Yasmin asleep, her bedside lamp still on, the book on the floor where it had dropped. Stiffly she walked over to the window and gazed out over the sleeping city. She stood with her face pressed against the cold plaster, and it was true what she had said to Kasseem; she hadn't been consciously crying then, but she did now, sobbing with her whole body for what had been lost. Finally, still standing pressed against the cool, brick wall, the tears, the racking sobs died, and she put up both hands to wipe at her wet face.

She wouldn't cry again; it was finished. And as she moved, her glance passing the window, she saw, low on the horizon, over a city that was coming awake, the first pink flush of colour from a rising sun. Was Kasseem back in this city which belonged to him? A smile, tinged with the bitterness of aloes, appeared for an instant on her pale lips. She supposed so. He was leaving Cairo too, today. She walked tiredly along to the bathroom, shutting the door to avoid waking Yasmin.

She turned the hot tap full on and undid the strings of the long white cloak. Shrugging it off, she dropped it into the wastepaper basket. Her lovely spoilt blouse followed, so too did the golden sheen of the skirt. It was not ripped and torn, but she would never wear it again. It would always bring memories of a hand that had trailed over it in passion, but not in love.

Bra and pants followed, so did the sandals. Her watch came off; then her hand, outstretched to send it after the other discarded articles, halted. No, she would never wear it, but it *had* been given to her with love and tenderness. For a moment Kasseem was standing before her as he had that first time she had seen him in Western clothes, on the roof-garden of this hotel.

She shook her head to clear it, and stepped quickly under the hot water, allowing its soothing warmth to banish some of the tension. Even her hair came in for its share of scrubbing. She wanted no part of her imprinted with last night's seal. Wrapped in a large towel, she went across to the window, rubbing her hair in the hot sunshine now spilling through it.

Whatever had happened last night, the day had to be lived through; a plane had to be caught, and self-respect made it necessary to at least look respectable. Her almost dry hair went into rollers. Opening her case, she pulled out from the very bottom a pair of jeans worn and washed to a faded blue. Told not to wear trousers in Egypt, she had left them unpacked. Today, she didn't care, and in four hours she would be leaving.

There was no way she was going upstairs to the big, bustling dining-room. She couldn't face it; and she couldn't face, either, a breakfast looking up at her. She would have a tray of tea and toast sent down. She stepped into the jeans and a plain white cotton blouse, and glancing into the mirror saw

suddenly superimposed, in its place, lemon crêpe-de-
chine.

She swung round as a sound came from Yasmin's
bed, glad of the interruption. The little girl was sitting up in bed staring at her. Heavens, she thought,
realising she was not looking her best, that her face
showed no colour, that the grey eyes held a heaviness
never before clouding them—she shouldn't have
brought that stare from Yasmin.

'What's the matter, love? Ups-a-daisy now! Time
for your bath—come along.'

'You do look funny, Aunty Alex. You have men's
trousers on.'

'Oh. . . .' Of course Yasmin would not have seen
women in trousers in her part of the world.

'No, Yasmin, these are what are called jeans. Girls
and ladies wear them in Australia all the time. I'll
tell you what—the first spare day we have, I'll take
you in and buy you some. How about that?'

No glad cries came from the small figure, but
shyly, words did. 'I don't know, Aunty Alex. You
look so funny.'

'Do I, love? Never mind, you'll get used to them.
Up now, and I'll turn on the shower for you. You
have to dress for the plane as well as for breakfast,
you know.'

Dressed and ready, Alex walked with her to Miss
Maitland's room. There they found Raschid.

'Oh, here you are, Alexandra,' Miss Maitland
greeted her. 'Just look at all this mess! I don't know
how it gets this way. . . .'

'There's a few hours yet before we leave; they'll be
ready. I was going to ask you, though, will you have
a tray of tea and toast sent down to my room. I have
a bit of a headache, and don't feel like going up.'

The older woman swung round, and deliberately not glancing her way, yet Alex felt the searching look she was being subjected to. 'You don't look well, that's true. For heaven's sake, Alexandra, don't get sick until we're out of here!' She looked affronted when Alex laughed. 'Well, you know what I mean. I simply couldn't face having to unpack all over again.'

'Would there really be anything to unpack?' Alex replied dryly, gesturing to the disarray all around them. 'But you go to breakfast, I'll have that tray in my room and finish up there, then come and deal with this.' On her way out, she saw she was the subject of another intent gaze, and it came from Raschid. She didn't look his way. *He* wasn't getting any explanation!

She drank all the tea, ate some of the toast, and finished their packing. The suitcases locked, her overnight bag on top of them, Alex checked the room, then taking Yasmin by the hand, left. It was no use looking back. All memories of this place had to be forgotten.

In Miss Maitland's room, there was no time to think of memories. It was pandemonium. Finally she went to knock on Raschid's door. 'Yes, Alex?' he said. 'Do you want me?'

'Yes, I do. Will you get your aunt and take her away—I'll never get the packing done with her there. Take her down to pay the account. That will keep her occupied, fighting with the accountant.'

He smiled, but followed her back, and it was his diplomacy that drew his aunt from the disordered room, still giving orders over her shoulder as she went. Heaving a sigh of relief, Alex set about getting into two cases what probably should be packed into three.

'There, Yasmin,' she told the little girl who had sat quietly as good as gold. 'All finished. Come along.' The head porter was at the corridor station. Alex smiled at him, and taking out all her remaining Egyptian money, placed it on the table. 'For everyone,' she said.

He bowed, saying, 'You are leaving Egypt, miss?'

She looked straight at him. It wasn't the question; it was the way it had been spoken. Of course she would see nothing in that face. She wondered what the talk was among the staff. She only said, 'Yes, I leave Egypt in a few hours. I'm sorry. I didn't expect to leave it.' There, she thought, make what you like of that.

She walked away from him, down the lifts for the last time, and holding Yasmin's hand, she walked across the huge marble floor.

And for the last time here too, she thought, as they made their way through the crowded, vociferous airport, their entourage of porters following with the luggage. In a daze now, feeling nothing, not even tiredness, Alex attended to what had to be done, then leant back in her seat, eyes closed.

'I don't believe it!'

Alex jerked herself up from her leaning position. 'What, Miss Maitland? What is it you don't believe?'

'The plane is late! They've just announced it. It was late in Athens. We shouldn't have to put up with it again!'

'It's only half an hour, Aunt,' put in Raschid. 'That's not too bad, and they will be calling us soon to go to the embarkation lounge.'

'Well, it's to be hoped we don't miss our connection in Athens. We go by Qantas from there, you know, and that airline doesn't run late.'

Walking behind her as they were called prior to take-off, Alex smiled, albeit a little tiredly. Qantas was their own Australian airline, and like others, it could also be late, but she didn't mention that to her companion.

And in the event, they didn't miss their connection. They had flown over Cairo, but from her window Alex could distinguish nothing—not even the Pyramids. Now, Yasmin beside her, with Miss Maitland and Raschid opposite, Alex settled down in her own seat, able to think her own thoughts at last. Outside the small window there were only clouds around them. It was already evening, and would soon be dark. The next stop was Colombo, then Singapore, then home.

Emerging from the doze into which she had dropped, and glancing out, Alex saw lights and realised they were descending. She noticed also that the faintness of a dawn just beginning was edging away, if slowly, the darkness of night. It was Singapore rising to meet them, and she decided that even with two small children, they had had a good trip.

All of them left the plane to stretch their legs, Miss Maitland hobbling along on her stick, holding on to Raschid's arm. She had slept, thank goodness, thought Alex, after swallowing the sleeping pill Raschid had insisted upon. Around them the sunshine they had become accustomed to had disappeared, vanishing even as they walked into a deeper grey overcast. 'Are you warm enough, love?' she asked the little girl skipping along beside her.

Yasmin's clothes had their origin in Egypt, and

possibly were not warm enough for her, at this season of the year. Still, they would be home in seven hours and all that could be taken care of then. Alex sighed. All she wanted was for this interminable journey to end; to get away and try to sort some order into her life.

Raschid waved a hand as a steward beckoned, and turning, they trooped once more up the steps, Alex this time helping the nurse with her carry-cot, Yasmin counting in Arabic as she jumped each step before them. Engines roared, and Alex watched yet another city slide behind her. Then there was only tossing water, and then not even that; just greyness and clouds closing them in.

Breakfast arrived to pass some of the time. Yasmin fell asleep and Alex made her comfortable. She dozed and read—or at least looked at the magazine she held, and then, unexpectedly, the sea was visible again, and farther away, the brown outline of land showed, and they were losing height. Trickles of rain were sliding against their window. Welcome home, thought Alex sardonically. Blue skies could have been there to greet them. She needed all the outside help she could get.

'Why is that water on the window, Aunty Alex?' Yasmin wanted to know as she gazed at the dribbles of water following one another down the window.

'That, my love, is rain. Even in Egypt you must have seen it sometimes.'

'Sometimes there's a big storm that frightens you, not a lot of them, though. But we never have soft little bits like that,' the small voice said.

'Well, that kind of rain makes all the grass and flowers grow, you'll see. Oh, look, Yasmin, there's Brisbane down there.' Both together the two heads, one blonde, one black, looked out of the window as the city below them drew nearer.

Mrs Benson was there to meet them when they finally got through Customs. Miss Maitland was furious that all their suitcases had been searched. 'To think of me being treated like that in my own town!' she kept saying. But they *had* come from the East, and they could have been anybody.

They tumbled into the two taxis Mrs Benson had waiting for them, Alex with the nurse and baby. It was strange driving along familiar streets which had seemed far away this last month. Luxor and Cairo had been the familiar settings then.

Taking Mrs Benson aside once they got to the big house on the hill, Alex said, 'I'd get Miss Maitland to bed straight away if you don't think it presumptuous of me to suggest it, Mrs Benson. She's had a long couple of days.' Relieved at getting a nod of complete agreement, she continued, 'Also, if you don't need me, I'd like to get along home.'

The housekeeper looked her over. 'And if you don't think I'm being presumptuous, Alex, I'd tell you to go home and go to bed yourself. You look awful. Of course we don't need you. I've had everything ready for days. The little girl is a charmer, isn't she?'

'She is,' answered Alex softly. 'She really is. But it's the baby boy who's stolen Miss Maitland's heart. Still, Yasmin holds Raschid's, so it will work out. Goodness, I'm tired!' And suddenly, she found she was.

'The keys are in your car, food in the fridge' said Mrs Benson. 'I went over yesterday and opened up for you. Off you go now.'

Alex knelt down beside Yasmin, giving her a quick

hug. 'I'll see you tomorrow, love,' she said.

'Don't you live here, Aunty Alex?' Yasmin sounded forlorn.

'No, I don't, but I live only a little way away, so I'll see you often.' She turned to the old lady who had been her constant companion for so long. 'I expect I have your full permission to go home and get sick, now that we've left Egypt?' she asked sweetly, then grinned at the outraged face and flipped a hand both to her and Raschid. She went out and down the verandah steps to dump her case and holdall into the back of her little Mini. Heavens, how small it was when she remembered. . . Shrugging, she turned the key. She was home now, she would just live and take one day at a time as it came along.

## CHAPTER THIRTEEN

'Oh miss, could you tell me . . .?'

Her arms full of books, Alex turned. 'I think down there,' she answered, and unable to point, led the way. 'Just try among that lot. I'll get rid of these and come back.' She slotted the dozen or so novels in their places, and returned. At least one satisfied borrower, she acknowledged to herself, as the particular book was located.

She went back for more of the returned copies, and as she put them on the shelves, she realised that it was Thursday today, and that tomorrow she would have been back at work a whole fortnight. The days had slipped away, and after a time she found she was eating a little better, and actually getting to sleep before the early hours of the morning.

It had rained for three days after they arrived home, but was back to the usual sunshine now. She saw a lot of Yasmin, because somehow the little girl gave her comfort—but almost nothing of Raschid. He was learning the business of running property; he seemed contented here and in his quiet way was creating a happy family up there on the hill.

The slightest sign of a smile showed itself for an instant. She had bought Yasmin her jeans and was rewarded by the delight they bestowed. Yasmin had taken to them like a duck to water. Alex herself would become one of that family if she didn't watch out—and that she didn't want. She had other plans.

Collecting another load of books, she turned from the counter, and they crashed to the floor. She stood there, colour fled from her face, hands and body shaking as they had on another occasion.

Kasseem said, 'I'll pick these up. Go and tell them you have to leave.'

She didn't move. The voice that spoke again could have been Ahmed's at his most dictatorial. 'I'll collect these. Either tell them, or you'll come without!' He bent down to reach for the scattered books.

Alex turned, unable to think, and gave the first excuse she could think of. 'May I go home?' she asked her superior. 'I think I'm going to be sick.' That was almost not a lie anyway.

'You don't look well, Alex,' he answered sympathetically. 'Yes, of course go.'

Collecting her handbag, Alex walked back again through the library. Kasseem was waiting by the door. Outside she turned, facing him. 'What are you doing here? What do you want?' she demanded.

'I have a taxi waiting. Is there a restaurant or some place where we can go? I have to talk to you!'

She looked helplessly up at him. All she could say was, again, 'Why are you here?'

'Take a grip on yourself, Alexandra. You look as if you are going to fall over.'

That did register. Drawing a deep breath, she told him, 'I don't know of any restaurant around here. This is a suburb, you know, not the city proper.'

'Where do you live? Can we go there?'

'No!' Panic coloured the tone.

'Don't be silly. Would I be here if I hadn't had time to think about that—night?.' It was in Arabic, that descriptive adjective, and Alex had no way of knowing what it meant.

Her head went from side to side. It was the shock, actually seeing him in the flesh—one didn't count dreams. Never had she expected him to come here.

He was piloting her towards the waiting taxi, she was half hanging back, unwilling to go. 'Your address?' he asked, his tone peremptory.

Alex gave it. The cab didn't start. The driver leaned over the seat, and asked. 'You all right, miss?' and his glance, with no sign of friendliness, went to Kasseem.

Did he think she was being abducted by a white slaver? thought Alex, and somehow that broke the tension. She smiled at him, and it held some of her normal warmth. 'Yes,' she told him, 'I am now. I had a shock at meeting an old friend.'

She wondered what Kasseem would say if he had read the driver's mind. Inwardly, she grinned. Heavens, the mighty Sheikh Kasseem ben Omair suspected of that! It was just a few minutes' drive to her unit up on the hill behind the Maitland house.

She got out and walked the few steps to the door as Kasseem paid off the taxi, waving away what must have been change proffered to him.

Through the small hallway, and into the lounge, she went to slide open the windows. The front door closed decisively. They stood looking at one another, and suddenly her heart lurched. It was no good saying such things did not happen; she had felt it.

'Alexandra. . . .'

She shook her head. He was so handsome, so wanted, so remembered. In fawn slacks and sports coat, and the white cashmere roll-neck sweater, which here in Australia made his dark skin seem even darker, it was no wonder the taxi-driver had asked if she wanted to go with him. He looked like someone out of the high-flying jet-set one read about in the colour supplements—and he had an accent. He certainly didn't look like the average Australian, and he certainly didn't act it, either.

She giggled suddenly and his eyebrow climbed in autocratic surprise at the unexpected sound. 'I was just wondering what the taxi-driver would have said if you'd come to collect me in your Arab clothes.'

There came the smallest of answering smiles on those austere lips. 'In my life, which takes me all over the place, it is de rigueur to accept that when in Rome one does as the Romans do. Now. . . .'

Before he could continue, Alex asked again, 'Why have you come?'

'I think that should be obvious.'

'It isn't obvious to me at all. Nothing has changed since the last time we were together.'

'No, nothing has. And don't think I have the slightest intention of apologising for any behaviour I indulged in. I thought I had every right to act as I did.'

'Well then!' Alex had straightened, the glance she was directing at him one of hostility.

'But even then, under it all,' Kasseem was continuing, unheeding her interjection, 'I knew that you were you, the woman I wanted, that I loved, and who also, I knew with certainty, loved me in return.'

'If you knew that, you still knew it when you came to Ahmed's tent and. . . .'

'I did, and I suppose that is why in the end I sent you home. Ahmed waited for me that morning, you know. I was still in a towering rage, I wasn't thinking clearly and I didn't consider his dignity, his pride. I treated him like one of my men out in the desert, simply to obey and not to question. He walked out!

'Still, my project was a success—my brother Khalid was engaged to the girl who was being thought of for me. I encouraged them to see the way my wife would have to live—will have to live. There will be few amenities of civilisation, at times, anyway. They were very happy to decide on Khalid. . . .'

'I bet they were,' she interrupted. 'I can imagine the parts you showed them. I know how you act when you want something. Talk about Ahmed!'

Kasseem was continuing as if she hadn't spoken. 'My brother, as I was saying, is clever, a rising young politician, and richer than I am—or so they thought.'

'And is he?' Acid coated the words.

'Are you interested, Alexandra? Would you like a husband who could drop gold and diamonds into your lap?'

There, that heart lurch came again, but all she said was, 'But of course I would be interested.

Diamonds and gold are what it's all about in the life of a houri of promiscuity. Surely someone like you who has had experience of them would know that!'

Across from her, instead of anger flying into those green eyes, amusement came, and that lopsided smile she had last seen at Karnak stretched his lips. 'Did I really say that to you, Alexandra? I'll tell you, though, the way I was feeling, you got off lightly.'

She didn't answer that smile; she said again, 'Why did you come? Beneath it all, Kasseem, some of the words you spoke carried truth. I *am* European. I *do* have different ideas of communication between the sexes. I could, not meaning to, do something again. . . .'

'I came because of Ahmed,' he told her. 'No, that is not true. I would have come anyway. But I knew I would have to make my peace with him. So, after reporting to the government the minute I got home, I sent Mustafa to him with a note. Do you know what he did? He sent Karim back informing me that he had only an hour left before leaving on his father's business. I knew what that meant, and I thought that two could play at that game. So I dressed in the formal clothes of a Sheikh of the ben Omair going to meet his paramount chief. I also gave him an obeisance lower than the one he gave to me on the launch at Luxor.

'He didn't unbend, but at least he sent away his six tribesmen and Karim who had stood at his back. We then spoke of my project and Khalid's betrothal—in Arabic, of course. Then suddenly he said, in English, 'You are a fool, Kasseem.'

'It was so unexpected. I was furious, of course I was. But it was the old Ahmed speaking, and he told me what you had said to him after he took you home

to the hotel. He also told me he didn't like the idea
of being the dark side of love's coin, and if I didn't
want you, he did!'

No words answered him, only a gasp from Alex,
and as Kasseem resumed, the words came silken as
she had heard them when his temper wasn't as
pleasant as it seemed now. 'So you *can* have a husband who can pour diamonds and gold into your
lap; Ahmed is richer than I am, and we are both
richer than Khalid; but then we are the Omair. . . .'

'The Omair . . . the Omair, I'm sick of hearing
the very sound of the word Omair! Oh,' aghast at
the unprecedented outburst, Alex's hand flew to her
mouth, 'I'm sorry, Kasseem.'

'That is too bad, Alexandra, because you will
belong to the Omair when you are married to me.'

This time she did close her eyes, and he was
suddenly in front of her, hands upon her shoulders.
Alex swayed against him, her feet on tiptoe, her arms
raised to clasp around his neck; her face upturned
for his kiss—and was stood away.

From only inches' distance they looked at one
another. 'I'm not starting that, Alexandra. I can't
take any more of these on-again-off-again love
scenes. Every time I begin to make love to you we
are interrupted.'

'And I can assure you that that won't be the case
this time.' Alex tried to make her voice like his had
sounded on that fateful night. 'You did say that to
me, Kasseem. I'm returning your words. I mean
them!'

'No!'

'I've missed you so.' Her words were barely a
whisper.

As if he couldn't help it, his head came down and

body melted into body, his arms bringing her more closely against him, as his searching lips sent passion running like a forest fire that blotted out the room, the space about them, everything. . . .

No, not everything; the man had pulled back, standing her free. 'Listen to me, Alexandra,' he said. 'We were getting married some time tomorrow. We leave for Egypt at five o'clock, where there will be another ceremony at Siwah, our capital.'

'How can we be getting married tomorrow? Have you been smoking hashish again, if you don't drink? And you're also looking at your damned watch again!'

He started to laugh, silently, as he sometimes did.

'Yes,' he acknowledged, 'that has been the story of our life, hasn't it, my love? I openly admit that time has been the enemy.'

Alex had heard the two words 'my love', the first time he had ever spoken an endearment in English. What he had said in Arabic was another matter. She only said, 'Well then, why can't you stay in Australia and get properly acquainted—and throw your rotten watch away?'

'Because I can't, and as for our wedding here, Miss Maitland is arranging it.'

'Miss Maitland?' The two words came out as a squeak.

'I found her number, and rang to find where you were. I got Raschid, and thank Allah he told that formidable old lady the whole story before I got there. I'd still be explaining it if he hadn't. She has set up what she calls fair exchange. She paid good Australian money, she informed me, to get those children out here—if I wanted to marry you tomorrow and take you to Egypt, she would have to have a powerful lever to obtain action so quickly. The upshot of it is that I donate a wall, or a roof, or whatever . . . and she'll see that there is a church, and a minister to officiate in it, and, from her lawyer—who has yet to be told—a special licence.'

'A minister?' Alex's voice had risen, and she allowed all the other rigmarole to slide for the moment. 'You told me you're a Moslem. How can you . . .?'

'Did I now? But that was a night for saying anything I could to frighten you. However, I *have* been inducted into the Mohammedan faith—but first I was christened in the Anglican church in Cairo. That was the only thing my mother insisted upon, and I have brought along all the necessary papers.'

'Kasseem,' Alex spoke slowly, 'you don't have to do all this. I don't care, except that I wouldn't want to become a Moslem.'

'My dear Alexandra, you flatter yourself. A mere woman doesn't need to become a Moslem. She lives under the protection of her husband. If he is one, naturally it is assumed she is one also.' He was laughing at her, but now his tone went curt. 'It won't affect you at all. Now come along, we are to go up to the Maitland house for lunch.'

Kasseem's hand reached out to lay over hers—in reassurance, she supposed. It must be that, because from that lunch at the Maitland home when they were running against time yet once again, to now, in this noisy helicopter, this husband who was not a husband had not so much as taken her by the elbow.

Still, her wedding might have been rushed, but Alex knew that remembrance of it would bring only warmth and happiness. Decorated with masses of flowers, the church had welcomed them; the reception held in the gardens of the Maitland home had come alive with her friends in pretty dresses and casual clothes. And goodness knows what the chatelaine of the house had said, or done, to obtain the gourmet lunch that had materialised at such short notice. Yasmin and Mrs Benson's four-year-old granddaughter had preceded her with baskets of flowers. And of course, it was Kasseem, tall and handsome, standing there so close by her side, who made her vitally aware that this very moment of existence meant happiness.

They had changed planes at Bahrein, and were met at Cairo by Khalid. Kasseem was looking at his watch again, Alex noted and was infuriated when after exchanges in Arabic, Kasseem informed her from yards away that she would be escorted to his brother's house, that he had affairs to attend to.

'Would you like me to just creep away somewhere and hide?' she asked him sweetly, and received that lopsided smile which she was becoming to know meant everything was all right in his own particular world. One thing she didn't want to experience again was the silken tone of threat that brought only alarm to her metabolism.

Taken up wide marble stairs and told to rest, she lay down—and slept the whole night through. Awakened by Kasseem in the morning, she had swung herself upright and gazed from his immaculate person to her own dishevelled figure, still in yesterday's clothes.

He smiled, and the expression on her face said it all. 'A quick shower and breakfast will make us equal,' he told her mockingly. 'And oh,' as he made

to depart, he added, 'we will be in Siwah this evening for the second ceremony. You do realise that?'

Alex nodded, a knot of fright tightening her
nerves. 'Are you wearing Western clothes, Kasseem?'
she asked.

That smile came again. 'By the sound of your
voice, one would think we were going into a lion's
den! These are my people, Alexandra. They will
welcome us both. And do you really imagine I go
around dressed up in formal white all the time? I
take leave to inform you that what you will most see
me in are khaki shirts and trousers, which quite likely
will be sweaty and dirty as well. I am a working
man, an engineer, and there is a lot of work waiting
for me to get on with.'

'Will that dress I wore in Brisbane be all right to
wear today?' She had deliberately chosen what she
thought would be suitable for Egypt, thick cream
crêpe with long full sleeves. Dropping from her
shoulders, it was caught tight around her slender
waist with a wide belt.

An eyebrow went up. 'I thought you looked
beautiful then, I see no reason for me not to think
you will look just as beautiful today. And don't flash
that damn smile at me,' he added, as at his words,
her face lit up. 'I'm off. You have half an hour.'

Now, as his hand pointed downwards, unable to hear
anything through the ear-plugs on her head, Alex
looked, amazed. She had thought that journey's end
would be an oasis; trees around a waterhole, albeit a
big one. This down here was a town they were flying
towards, with buildings and trees and squares. They
were dropping quickly, and it wasn't only the motion
that provided that empty feeling. Kasseem was

easing off her ear-plugs, and as they stopped, he had jumped out, turning to help her. Outside, she gazed quickly around. It was almost like Ahmed's film-set tent. Drawn up were horsemen, with two out in front, one a pace behind. As she and Kasseem walked across to them, they dismounted as one man.

'This is Alexandra,' was all Kasseem said. 'My uncle, the Sheikh Hassan ben Omair.'

Gazing at that dark bearded face, Alex found no reassurance. It looked directly back at her. She couldn't hold out a hand; she couldn't say 'How do you do'. She dropped a curtsy.

The face smiled, Alex saw the flash of white, and a voice from out the bearded face said in heavily accented English, 'Welcome.'

'And welcome also from me, Alex,' said a gay voice. Thankfully she turned, half holding out a hand before pulling it back just as quickly. Ahmed laughed. 'Did my cousin tell you what I said to him not very long ago?'

Alex felt the blood mount to her face, but she answered demurely enough. 'Yes, I was told what my husband's cousin had said. I would like to thank him and say the words gave me moral reassurance.'

Again a laugh erupted from the young, autocratic face, but he stepped back a pace behind his father, who was signalling. Of all things, a jeep made its appearance. Amazement brought Alex's gaze round to Kasseem. He had raised a finger—goodness, were they back to old times? thought Alex—and their luggage was being taken from the pilot and being dropped into the back of their khaki-coloured conveyance. Escorted by two rows of trotting horsemen, their entry into the town of Siwah was a progress.

There was movement and people, and shops and

bazaars, and buildings built of something like white stone, some of them quite large, and of course, the ubiquitous palm-trees. Their jeep went through a wide aperture, from which great doors were folded back. It passed the main façade of what seemed like some Eastern palace and stopped in a tree-lined cul-de-sac. Alex was handed out, and suddenly there was a bevy of women around her. They were dressed in roomy white overdresses, but their faces were bare. No veils were in evidence, and their features weren't being hidden from the driver and Kasseem, thought Alex in relief.

Unheard-of before in public, Kasseem had taken her hand. 'Will you do as they tell you, Alexandra? It will be for our ceremony, which is to begin at six o'clock. You will not have to do anything, just be there, and dressed as our women are dressed.'

She didn't want to go; she didn't want him to leave her. She gazed into his green eyes and knew suddenly what she had to do. 'Yes, my lord,' she answered, and turned away.

An older woman was clearly in charge, but a young girl spoke English and, Alex noticed, astonished, with a very upper-class accent. It was this person who smiled shyly at Alex, and said, 'My name is Lallah and I will speak for you. You will have your bath first, then dress, please.' Afterwards, Alex knew things began to run into one another. She had been flying for almost three days, had left Cairo this morning and flown to Luxor, to be met by a deputation headed by Kasseem's father—with whom, Alex smiled to herself in congratulation, she had got on very well—then on to this place in a noisy, clamouring helicopter. Now she glanced at her watch, which Kasseem—no, her husband, had brought for her, which showed it was after four o'clock.

She was led into a room covered with shining tiles. In the centre of this was sunk a huge bathtub. Sharply, speaking in Arabic, the older woman was obviously giving orders. Alex eyed the large tub somewhat askance, but Lallah told her gently, 'It is the custom, just to prepare you for your marriage.'

Shrugging, Alex allowed the Australian wedding dress to be removed, and to a running commentary of soft words from Lallah, was bathed, then brought to lie upon what looked like a slotted marble table. On this she was pummelled, then massaged with a paste which did bring a protest from her. 'I don't want a heavy perfume rubbed all over me,' she told Lallah.

'It is attar of roses; it is very nice,' explained Lallah from where she was sitting at Alex's head. 'It is always used for brides.'

'Where did you learn to speak such beautiful English, Lallah?' asked Alex. Suddenly she had found she was lying there relaxed, at peace with the world.

'We have a school here. A man and a woman from England teach us. Every child, boy or girl, must learn; we are also taught other things besides English. We have a hospital too, but only for men; and women who have been married are allowed to be taught nursing.' There was regret in the gentle voice. 'I would like to be a nurse, but it is thought by our elders to be not suitable for young girls.'

Of course it would not be suitable here; no young Arab girl of good family would be allowed to be exposed to what nursing meant.' I didn't think I'd find schools and hospitals so far away from established cities,' said Alex, as she was turned over yet once again.

'The lord Graham, the grandfather of the lord Kasseem, began all these things a long time ago. We had water, but not a lot, you understand.' Here, Lallah glanced anxiously at Alex's prone face. 'He was very clever and brought in big things ... big machinery, I think you call it. Now there's plenty of water. Just like my lord Kasseem who is trying to bring it to our dry oases in the far desert.'

'It really is all so different from what I expected,' confessed Alex. 'I didn't imagine this, or being prepared for a wedding as I am being.'

'The massage is an old custom ... very old,' said Lallah, throwing out an arm to describe a distance farther and farther away. 'It has come down to us from long years ago. We all learn, but only some are allowed to be mistresses of it.' She moved away as Alex was gestured to rise. She smelt it as she moved—a fragrance, the true perfume of roses, as if she were carrying them against her.

But there was one thing she knew she would not like. Being dressed like an Arabian dancer in trousers and a gossamer top was in the first category, but she had promised. She need not have worried. A muslin shift was dropped over her head, like the material she had felt when close to Kasseem.

As she sat on a stool, her hair was brushed, and yet a different woman came to take charge of it. It was like a union, each to his own. More stuff from a pot was used, her hair was twisted up on top of her head, with one lonely curl hanging down over one cheek. Moreover, it stayed in place, which was more than Alex could ever make it do, and was the reason she wore it so simply, just brushed and held back with combs. It must be that mixture which was being used.

'You must keep your eyes still.' Almost an admonishing tone came into Lallah's gentle voice, as yet another woman was painting around and beneath Alex's eyes. She tried to obey, but by now was beginning to wonder what on earth she would look like when they had finished with her. This thought went farther as her lips were brushed, not with the familiar lipstick, but with a liquid.

Standing up once more, she heard a twittering of excited voices from her audience, who had remained to watch, and comment, as Alex had heard.

She slid her arms into the garment being held for her, and saw it was a kind of a coat—and it was beautiful. Made of what seemed a very heavy linen, it had a four-inch border of embroidery down the front of both sides where it met. Sleeves to her wrists had the same border ornamentation. Blue and gold, cerise and magenta, green and purple; the colours glowed, each one a separate entity.

Lallah was securing not buttons, but a toggle-like fastening which slipped into loops. The older woman who had stood apart, speaking only to give orders, pointed, and a pair of sandals fashioned seemingly only of straps with the same magnetic colours that enhanced her coat were fastened about her ankles.

'Come,' said Lallah. Alex followed her over to an alcove against a far wall and looked. She didn't recognise the face gazing back at her from out of the mirror. It was a different Alex altogether. Her fringe was all that remained of the image that had walked in here; and even that had been swept sideways to become much shorter. The rest of her hair except for that one piece cascading down her neck was twisted into intricate folds and swirls on top of her head. And heavens, she thought, no eyeshadow could do what they had done to enhance her eyes. They looked enormous, and her lips, as if stained with raspberry juice, were exactly delineated. She was beautiful.

If all this could be done here in what passed for the wilderness, what price modern cosmetics? She shook her head at the startling lovely girl gazing back at her, because under it all, Alex knew she was only a bit better-looking than average.

'Come,' called Lallah again, and down a corridor and into a room she was ushered. This one had all the appearance of being lived in, with couches and cushions, tables and chests, and in its centre stood a woman, unseen until now. She smiled, and translating her words, Lallah said, 'The wife of the Sheikh Hassan bids you welcome, and presents you with the wedding present of the Omair.'

Alex bowed, she didn't know what else to do, saying, 'Thank her for me, Lallah,' then was silent as a box was proffered, and from it emerged a shimmer of gold. The woman moved forward to place it over Alex's head, and a gasp escaped her.

She had thought it was just a golden chain, but there on her breast, intricately set in heavy gold, flashed what looked like a diamond, scintillating and sending off brilliance when the slightest movement caused it to catch the light. But, suddenly reassured, she smiled. It was probably some lesser stone, or even perhaps something created in the bazaar. A diamond this size certainly wouldn't be given away with such little ceremony.

All the women turned now towards an arched entrance, and Lallah motioned Alex before her, and from now on events began to disintegrate into a kaleidoscope of noise and colour. With Alex in their midst, the women settled on a raised dais in the square fronting the palace. From a farther side came a small coterie of men, Kasseem among them. He was seated beside Alex, but some feet away. For the briefest moment he looked at her, and an eyebrow went as high as it could go, a complacent smile accompanying it. His gaze, dropping farther, took in the bauble upon her breast. There was no indication either way that he had noticed it, except that that smile deepened.

Horses and riders were doing incredible exercises out there before them, and with her heart in her throat Alex was glad that the man at her side was anchored there, and that it was Ahmed sitting next to him. She had no doubt that they both could do, and had done, what was being performed, among the dust, the bright lights, and the shouting.

Then came jugglers, and dancing girls, but not dressed like the one Alex had seen at the night-club in Cairo. There was food, all the time, of which she ate as little as she could get away with.

Then, unexpectedly, in all the commotion, entertainment was gone, and into the silence one person was speaking. He was speaking before them, Alex realised, and sat perfectly still, her head lowered. Was this the Mullah? A great shout went up, and Kasseem smiled across at her. 'I expect,' she muttered to herself a trifle acidly, 'he really considers himself married now.'

He was standing; she too was on her feet, and pulling up in front of them was the funniest-looking vehicle Alex had seen, riding on great, wide balloon-tyres. 'We're leaving, Alexandra,' she was told. Just like that.

'Don't I say goodbye? Don't I thank anyone?' she

was asking. What did one do in this unknown situation?

'All you do is obey your husband. Into here now!'

'Very well. In all my wedding finery, if you say so.'

And again she was riding across the desert; but not on a horse, and not with Ahmed. The man sitting beside her was driving, remote, silent, as was Mustafa in the back seat. All Alex could do was what she was doing, looking out at the scene flying past. A crescent of pale moon was up in the sky; not flooding the desert sands with brilliant silver as a full one had once flooded the Nile waters for her, but it was there, putting the stars to shame.

And then, as once before, a flash of brightness flickered low upon the horizon. Yes, there it came again, and in minutes they were among trees and buildings. These they passed, to pull to a stop before a tent—a very large one, Alex saw, standing within a group of palms on the fringe of the oasis.

'This is my headquarters for the present, Alexandra. Later, more permanent accommodation will be built.' He didn't help her down; he reached in and swung her up into his arms. In two strides he had stood her down inside the lighted tent. This was as different from Ahmed's as it could be. It was a place in which one lived and worked. A desk, cluttered with papers, having a straight-backed European-style chair before it, took up a far side. Seeing it, Alex was happy, but she followed somewhat slowly as Kasseem hooked back the canvas dividing the big tent. The bedroom was almost as austere as the outside living space. A large bed, a heavy carved hanging-press, some carved chests and a bedside table completed the furnishings. Oh, and a carpet, she saw, thinking of another much more beautiful one.

'Not at all like Ahmed's,' she said contentedly, gazing around   and heard the outside flap drop.

'But it can be used for the same purpose as Ahmed's was intended that night,' the voice behind her said. Kasseem turned her round, and looking deep into the green brilliance that his fully opened lids disclosed, Alex swayed against him, closing her own eyes. His arms were about her, one spreadeagled against her back, melting curve into curve. On tiptoe, which came to her so naturally, arms clasped around his neck, her own arched backwards as his lips travelled slowly down from temple to throat.

Lifting her, he swung her to the bed, and moving to the table turned out the light. The toggled fastenings came undone easily and Kasseem lifted the coat and threw the lovely thing on to the night table. 'Do you know, my love,' his soft words came from against her lips, 'I can't make myself believe I am here, alone with you, and that someone won't come barging in. But tonight no one would get past Mohammed, so I can. . . .'

'Weren't "indulge yourself" the words you used?' asked Alex sweetly.

The form beside her, holding the length of her body so tightly against his own, rippled, and Alex thought, satisfied, he's laughing, he must be happy— and then abruptly, she wasn't thinking, she was being kissed. And all the love-scenes with this man before hadn't prepared her for the storm of emotion he was now calling up; for this blaze of desire mounting higher and higher, as his caresses flamed the darkness around her with crimson.

Later she lay, unwilling to sleep, not wanting to

let this night drift into yesterday. The faintest illumination from outside showed the space around her
dimly outlined. Kasseem, at her side, was asleep, she
thought, listening to breathing that had eased down
to normal. Softly she said, 'My lord.'

'Yes?' he answered immediately, and his voice
showed no sign of drowsiness.

'And you answer to it automatically! Does everyone call you that?'

'It's just a title, Alexandra. Like people saying sir
in England to their boss.'

'I can imagine them saying sir, but not in the
tone of voice that Mustafa and Lallah and all the
others say my lord. And as you *are* awake, will you
tell me what to do with this bauble I was given
tonight? It looks like something from the bazaars
which tourists buy and then take home and throw
into a drawer.'

The form resting alongside the length of her body
rippled for the second time that night. 'Oh, I don't
think you had better do that. I was pleased though
to see it on you—not that I couldn't provide you
with one myself—because it meant that my uncle
had accepted you.'

'It isn't ... it really isn't a proper diamond—
Don't be funny Kasseem! It would be worth a king's
ransom if it were.'

'It probably is—worth a king's ransom, I mean.
And I want you to wear it, just where it lies now.'
His fingers came out of the dimness to feel where the
pendant was resting. Her body jumped, and the
ripple had shifted from body to laughing voice as
Kasseem recognised the response his touch had en-
gendered.

'It is a diamond, Alexandra, but I don't want you

to talk about it outside. Diamonds are the origin of the Omair wealth. Carefully and slowly down through the years they have been mined in a country a long way from here. When my uncle gives his permission I will tell you about it. For now,' his hand trailed down her hip as it had once before across a golden yellow skirt —but there was no golden yellow skirt impeding his touch now  then slowly returned up and across her body. His lips came down softly, caressing her's with a sweet slowness that changed to quickened passion as she was gathered yet closer against the tensile length of a body that was Kasseem's. And this, somewhere inside her a voice was saying, is the bright side of love's coin.

# *Harlequin®* Plus
## A WORD ABOUT THE AUTHOR

When Mons Daveson was a girl, her family moved from England to the remote and sparsely settled Australian Outback. Mons loved the open spaces, and when she left the area, she reflects, ''I left behind a part of me.''

Her home is now in Brisbane, a bustling city on Australia's east coast, and her writing desk sits before an expanse of windows that affords a view of the whole city.

With a family and house to look after, Mons says she doesn't have unlimited time at her disposal for writing. ''But if by chance I reach a part in my story that is impossible to leave, I'm afraid such extraneous and mundane chores as housekeeping must go by the board!'' She hastens to add, though, ''I must admit I am a conscientious person, and dinner always does appear.''

Traveling is one of her greatest joys, and she has traveled all over Australia, especially in the Dead Heart, the popular name for the country's barren central region. ''The color and terrain are very different there from the coastal area,'' she points out. ''The coast has its color, too, but the shades of ocean and beach are so different from the colors inland that the two places could be on different planets.''

Mons Daveson's first attempt at romance writing met only with a publisher's rejection slip, but she was determined to persevere.

Why? Her answer is to the point. ''Because writing, as far as I am concerned, is something I must do.''